THE SPANIARD'S
VIRGIN
HOUSEKEEPER

Lexicon Library

Items that you have checked out

Title: A mansion and its murder.
ID: DLR20001010908
Due: 17/12/2021

Title: Into the woods / Virginia Andrews
ID: DLR210001011305
Due: 17/12/2021

Title: The Greek tycoon's Achilles heel / Lucy
        Gordon.
ID: DLR20002177701
Due: 17/12/2021

Title: The shy bride / Lucy Monroe.
ID: DLR200001445457
Due: 17/12/2021

Title: The Spaniard's virgin housekeeper /
        Diana Hamilton.
ID: BX001642209001
Due: 17/12/2021

Total items: 5

Account balance: 0.00 EUR
26/11/2021
Checked out: 6
Overdue: 0
Hold requests: 0
Ready for collection: 0

Thank you for visiting us today

THE SPANIARD'S VIRGIN HOUSEKEEPER

BY

DIANA HAMILTON

MILLS & BOON®

Pure reading pleasure™

First published in Great Britain 2008
Large Print edition 2009
Harlequin Mills & Boon Limited,
Eton House, 18-24 Paradise Road,
Richmond, Surrey TW9 1SR

© Diana Hamilton 2008

ISBN: 978 0 263 20588 6

Set in Times Roman 17 on 20 pt.
16-0509-45353

Printed and bound in Great Britain
by CPI Antony Rowe, Chippenham, Wiltshire

THE SPANIARD'S VIRGIN HOUSEKEEPER

BY

DIANA HAMILTON

MILLS & BOON®
Pure reading pleasure™

First published in Great Britain 2008
Large Print edition 2009
Harlequin Mills & Boon Limited,
Eton House, 18-24 Paradise Road,
Richmond, Surrey TW9 1SR

© Diana Hamilton 2008

ISBN: 978 0 263 20588 6

Set in Times Roman 17 on 20 pt.
16-0509-45353

Printed and bound in Great Britain
by CPI Antony Rowe, Chippenham, Wiltshire

CHAPTER ONE

ISABEL MAKEPEACE, mostly known as Izzy, sank down onto a bench beneath an arching tree that would shade her from the fierce midday Spanish sun and blinked furiously at the crystal-clear blue waters of the Atlantic. She would not cry. She would *not*!

Thrusting out her full lower lip, she huffed at the fall of gossamer-fine, silvery blond unmanageable hair that was obscuring her vision and wished she wasn't such a monumental failure—wished her feet didn't hurt so much when she could envisage having to walk miles and miles in search of somewhere dirt-cheap to stay while she looked for work.

Trouble was, being a scant five feet tall, she

always wore killingly high heels, no matter what. Distinctly lacking stature, in the height department she needed all the help she could get.

Not that her family had ever commented on that—to her—vitally important lack. Lacking in brains, as her much older brilliant brother had cuttingly remarked on more occasions than she cared to remember. And lacking in common sense, as her father would sigh in exasperation while her mother merely shook her head sadly at the daughter who had been a surprise late arrival. An unpleasant surprise, Izzy sometimes feared, while vowing to try harder to live up to her brilliant brother, who was the golden apple of her parents' eyes.

The phone line from New Zealand had crackled with her father's displeasure when she'd told him she had left her job back in England—the job, moreover, that he had created for her amongst, as she strongly suspected, opposition from the other senior partners—and was taking another as an

English-speaking mother's help to a wealthy Spanish couple in Cadiz.

He'd forecast that it would end in tears and he'd been right. It had.

The difference being she was not going to shed them!

The advertisement she'd seen in one of the national dailies had seemed heaven-sent. The successful applicant's duties would include looking after six-year-old twin girls and prac-tising English with them, plus a little light housework. It had seemed like the answer to her prayers—the perfect way to start a new life.

That she'd actually landed the job had been a huge boost to her self-esteem—especially after the humiliation dealt her by the man she had adored with more romantic yearning than good old-fashioned common sense. Determined to forget Marcus and her broken heart, to prove herself to be the best ever mother's help and to show big brother James and her long-suffering parents that she didn't fail at everything she turned her hand to, she'd embarked on her new career with energy and goodwill.

She'd cheerfully swallowed the fact that although her new employers, Señor and Señora del Amo, occupied a large, opulent villa on the outskirts of the city, the room she'd been given was not much larger than a cupboard, with a small skylight, an iron-hard narrow bed, and a rickety chest of drawers that she'd banged her shins on every time she'd had to squirm past it to get into or out of bed.

The twins had been a nightmare, refusing to do a single thing she asked of them, and pretending they understood not a single word of English when their mother had proudly claimed the opposite. They had given her either blank stares or shrill giggles when she had attempted, with the help of a phrasebook, to speak to them in their own language.

It had soon dawned on Izzy that she was regarded as a low-paid skivvy. Her day off had been cancelled more often than not, and the 'light housework'—piled onto her between taking the girls to school and escorting them home again—had translated into anything from sweltering over an Everest of ironing to scrubbing the marble paving of the immense entrance hall. But she'd got on with it because she'd been determined she wasn't going to walk out and admit yet another failure.

She had quickly learned to keep out of Señor del Amo's way as much as humanly possible because he—sixteen flabby stones of oiliness—had seemed to think that because he was a wealthy banker and paid her paltry wages he was entitled to paw her whenever he felt like it.

Izzy had made up her mind to save as much as she possibly could to fund her escape. She'd planned to save the means of paying her way on public transport to one of the busy holiday *costas*, where her poor grasp of Spanish wouldn't be a problem, and finding somewhere cheap to stay while she looked for work in a hotel or bar. But it was a plan that had rapidly hit the dust this morning, when Señor del Amo had sneaked up on her while she'd been loading the washing machine.

Struggling to extricate herself from what had seemed to be an octopus's complement of arms, she'd been unaware that the Señora had walked in on the torrid scene until a shrill stacatto of Spanish had brought merciful release. Rubbing her mouth with the back of her hand to rid it of the shudder-making assault of wet, blubbery lips, she hadn't even tried to translate Señor del Amo's response to his wife. But her pansy-blue eyes had sparked with outrage when the Señora had turned her hard black eyes on her and ordered, 'Get out of our home immediately! How dare you try to seduce an honorable family man—a husband and the father of two innocent girls?'

Stunned by the horrible injustice, Izzy had only been able to gasp with disbelief as her enraged employer had imparted with relish, 'From me you will have no references, and any money owing to you will not be paid. Your name will be forever linked with lewd behaviour among the civilised circles we move in!'

To have sprung to her own defence would have been a waste of breath, Izzy knew. Señora del Amo would believe what she wanted to believe, what made her feel comfortable, and even without looking at him she had known the Señor would be looking smugly triumphant.

There had been nothing for it but to pack her bags and go.

Looking on the bright side, she was glad to be away from the Señor's wandering hands and leery smiles, from the Señora's bossy, unrelenting demands and the terrible twins.

Her dignity restored, she had turned pitying eyes on the Spanish woman and told her, 'If you believe a word your husband says you're a bigger fool than I took you for.'

As Izzy had clipped out she'd almost felt daggers in her back, and she knew she'd made herself an enemy for life.

So here she was: no roof over her head, no

job, and little likelihood of landing one in Cadiz with her scant knowledge of Spanish and not enough money to get her to the nearest busy holiday resort, where the language barrier wouldn't be such a problem, and where there would be plenty of bars and hotels looking for staff at the height of the season.

She wasn't going to break into her pitifully few euros to phone her parents in New Zealand, where they'd moved to be with her brother on her father's retirement, and ask to be rescued. To have to admit to yet another failure would be the final straw.

Her small chin firming, Izzy gathered her suitcase and slung her rucksack over her shoulders. Something would turn up. Maybe someone in the dockland area wanted someone to clean offices. It was worth consulting her phrasebook and asking, wasn't it?

An hour later—still jobless, her feet killing her—Izzy left the fascinating commercial docks with their huge cargo vessels, busy tugs, gleaming cruise liners and little fishing boats behind her and headed towards the old town. She wandered through the maze of narrow shade-darkened streets, where projecting balconies almost met overhead, giving respite from the blazing heat, seeking a café where the price of a cold drink would be much lower than she could hope to find in the smarter, newer part of town.

The irritating mass of her hair was dragging in her eyes, and her cotton T-shirt and skirt were sticking to her overheated body. She wondered if she took her shoes off to give her poor feet a rest she'd ever get them back on again.

But her self-pity vanished as the only other occupant of the narrow street—a frail, shabbily dressed old man—tottered and collapsed. Concern tightening her soft mouth, Izzy dropped her luggage, ignored her protesting feet and sprinted forward to help.

His tough jaw set at a pugnacious angle, Cayo Angel Garcia descended from the penthouse suite he occupied when business demanded he spent time in Cadiz and exited the lift on the ground floor, instead of going down to the underground residents' car park and collecting the Merc.

He would walk—burn off some of his anger.

Impatiently he ran long tanned fingers through his short, expertly cut midnight hair and lengthened his stride, his dark eyes narrowed against the white light of the morning sun.

Returning briefly to the *castillo* after two months out of the country on business, he'd found amongst his personal post a letter from Tio Miguel. Skimming it, he'd felt the usual mixture of deep affection and exasperation. The old guy was the nearest thing to a real father he'd ever had. Cayo's own father, Roman, had wanted little to do with him, blaming him for the untimely death of his adored wife when his baby son had been barely two months old.

It had been Miguel who had shown him the only familial affection he had known—who had spent time with him, advised him. But when it came to taking advice Miguel closed his ears!

The elder of the two brothers, Miguel had inherited the vast family estates, while Roman had inherited the family-founded export empire—an empire Cayo had then inherited on his father's death five years ago.

Cutting across the busy Avenida del Puerto, he entered the narrow, warren-like streets of the old city. He blamed himself for not putting his foot down. Firmly. His uncle, a lovable old eccentric, owned vast wealth, but he insisted on living like a pauper in a mean dwelling, uninterested in what he wore or the food he ate—if he remembered to eat. His whole life revolved around his books. Cayo loved the old man dearly, but his unnecessarily austere lifestyle exasperated and worried him. He should have had him removed—forcibly, if necessary—to the *castillo*, where he would be looked after properly.

But, believing that a man had the right to live his life as he saw fit, providing he did no harm—and no man was more harmless and gentle than his uncle—Cayo had done nothing.

And look what had happened! Strong white teeth ground together in an excess of self-castigation.

The letter that had been waiting for him hadn't rung alarm bells. In fact he'd been pleased to learn that Tio Miguel had finally employed a new housekeeper. A young English girl, Izzy Makepeace, to take the place of the old crone who, it had always appeared to Cayo, had done little more than shuffle around the kitchen. And even there, he strongly suspected, she'd done nothing more energetic than lift a glass or six of manzanilla and spend time gossiping with the neighbours on the doorstep.

When Cayo had voiced a strong suggestion that the crone be given her marching orders it had brought the inevitable mild response. 'Like me, Benita is old. She can't be expected to leap around like a teenager. We manage well enough. Besides, she relies on me for a roof over her head.'

Therefore Cayo had been gratified to read that the crone had left, to be a burden on her probably unsuspecting grandson and his young wife, and that his uncle had managed to find a young woman to take over her duties.

Skipping over the neat copperplate paean praising the new paragon's general excellence, Cayo had thankfully said goodbye to his growing unease over his uncle's domestic arrangements.

Until.

Until last night.

Cayo had combined a visit to his offices in the commercial docks here in Cadiz with a tedious but necessary dinner with business associates, and had planned a long overdue and pleasurable visit to his uncle the following day.

He had sat through the dinner last night, hosted by the banker Augustin del Amo and his wife Carmela, wondering which of the city's fine restaurants would be most to his uncle's liking when he took him to lunch the following day—after Cayo had given the new housekeeper the once-over and made sure she knew her duties. First among these was the need to make sure the old gentleman ate regularly and well, of course. And then something said by the regrettably detestable Carmela del Amo had gained his full and riveted attention.

'It is impossible to get decent domestic help—my poor children have been without a nanny for over a month now, ever since we had to tell the last one to leave. Izzy Makepeace—an English girl. Such a mistake to hire her in the first place!' She had rolled her hard black eyes dramatically, managing to look martyred, and announced, 'I overlooked her slovenly laziness. I am a realist, and one cannot expect perfection no matter how much one pays. But when it comes to contaminating my dear, innocent girls I draw the line. The creature was little better than a *puta*.' Preening in the undivided attention of her guests, she had tipped her expertly coiffured head in her husband's direction. 'You know better than I, Augustin.'

The banker had looked smug as he'd leaned back in his chair, lifting his wine glass. 'You know how it is. Money is an aphrodisiac. I didn't dare be alone with her for one second— offered herself on a plate. For a financial consideration, naturally. If I'd been the type to take a mistress then I might have been tempted. A lush little package if ever I saw one!'

In receipt of a look that would have wilted an oak in the prime of life, he had added quickly, 'But, as I'm a faithful family man, I—we—told her to pack her bags and leave.'

The anger that had been building ever since he'd received that unwelcome information made Cayo feel as if he were about to explode. The smallest amount of research would have given his uncle's new housekeeper the information that Miguel Garcia—scholar and local eccentric—was, to use her probable terminology, filthy rotten rich.

Izzy Makepeace, with the morals of an alley cat, had successfully got her greedy claws in one of the kindest, most innocent old gentlemen ever to inhabit the planet. But he, Cayo Angel Garcia, was about to ensure that this situation was sorted out immediately!

Izzy Makepeace.

Make *war* was more like it!

CHAPTER TWO

'I'M BACK from market, *señor*,' Izzy announced cheerfully as she entered the cramped ground-floor room her new employer used as his study. A wayward strand of silky blond hair had escaped from the ribbon she'd used to anchor the unruly mass on top of her head, and she pushed it out of her eyes with the back of her hand. 'We have fresh-caught pilchards for lunch, and green beans.'

Cheap, but nourishing.

The housekeeping allowance was astonishingly small, and most of her unremarkable weekly wage went on supplementing it—but she wasn't complaining because her employer was so obviously poor and in no position to pay the going rate. It was immensely gratifying to see the old gentleman looking less frail than he had when she'd helped him when he'd fallen in the street, thankful that he spoke her language and had been able to direct her when she'd offered to see him to his home.

'And peaches—they looked so scrummy I couldn't resist!'

'Scrummy?' Miguel Garcia looked up from his seat at the desk that was half buried beneath tottering piles of books and papers, his lean, ascetic, once-handsome face breaking into a warm smile as he peered at her over the top of his spectacles, stuck together with sticky tape.

'Delicious.' Izzy grinned back at him, translating from the vernacular.

'Ah. I understand!' He leaned back in his chair, steepling his fingers, his dark eyes kind. 'Then I shall enjoy our lunch. While I think of it—I have asked you before, and as you've been with me for five weeks now I no longer ask. I *insist* you address me by my given name. Miguel. It will be more companionable.'

'Okay,' she agreed blithely. 'But only if you drop what you're doing and come out with me for a little fresh air and exercise.'

He was researching the life of some obscure saint or other, he'd told her, and it was her gladly embraced mission to ensure he remembered to eat and forgot his work long enough to take a short stroll each morning and evening.

'You bully me!' But his gentle smile as he laid down his pen told her he didn't object in the least. 'May I claim an old man's privilege and say how pretty you look this morning?'

'Oh!' Izzy's face was bright pink. He was good for her confidence—at one time flat on the floor! So good, in fact, that she no longer needed the boost of killingly high heels, and had bought flat sandals from the open-air market. She had to admit they made her feel as wide as she was high—but, hey, it made walking so much more comfortable!

And the old gentleman was so *grateful* for everything she did. She was sure he'd never noticed the squalor he lived in until she'd got rid of it—washing, scrubbing and polishing until the humble little house positively gleamed. The praises following his initial stunned surprise at the transformation had come thick and fast, making her head spin. Because she couldn't remember being praised for anything before in the whole of her twenty-two years.

Their separate guardian angels must have put their heads together on the day the del Amos had thrown her out and Señor Garcia had collapsed on the street. Both being in the right place at the right time had been really fortunate. The old gentleman was now looking much better, and she was thankful to have found a new job and a roof over her head so quickly, happy to be doing something worthwhile.

Remembering the ear-bending she'd received when she'd phoned her parents to tell them she'd quit her first job and landed another as a mother's help in Cadiz, she didn't want to repeat the experience. She had got around to writing last week instead, giving them her new address. That done, she wasn't going to think about the kind of nagging reply she'd get when she could enjoy being appreciated for once.

'I'll put the shopping away,' she told her employer, 'then we'll go out and enjoy the air before it gets too hot.'

Closing the study door behind her, she headed for the kitchen, her cool, brightly patterned cotton skirt swirling around her bare legs. She swung round as the street door opened to reveal a tall, dark stranger.

An impressively handsome stranger.

Her pansy-blue eyes widened as she took in his height and the breadth of shoulder beneath a stone-coloured fine cotton shirt tucked into the narrow waistband of obviously designer chinos. They clothed long, athletic legs, and ended in shoes that, at a guess, had to have been hand-made from the finest, most supple leather.

Slowly raising her eyes, she was stunned by the impact of sculpted high cheekbones, an aristocratic blade of a nose, and dark-as-night eyes fringed by lashes that were as soft and black as his expensively styled hair—eyes that were looking at her with blatant hostility.

'Izzy Makepeace?'

The beautiful, sensual male mouth curved with what she could only translate as derision. Her heart thumped a warning.

Who was he? Surely not a plain-clothes policeman, sent to arrest her because Señora del Amo had reported her alleged lewd behaviour, calling her a danger to all innocent children and middle-aged married millionaires in Cadiz—if not the whole of Spain? But policemen couldn't afford to dress in designer clothes that would have cost them the equivalent of a year's wages. Nor would they wear anything like the slim gold watch that banded his angular wrist—that would have cost them their pension!

Stifling hysteria—she mustn't let herself get

paranoid over the gross injustice done her by
the powerful del Amos—Izzy crossed her arms
defensively over her midriff, lifted her neat chin
and demanded, 'Who wants to know?'

And she cringed with helpless inadequacy as
he swept her a look of chilling contempt,
making her feel several centimetres short of
two inches tall.

'Cayo!'

At the sound of her employer's voice Izzy let
her tautly held spine relax just a little. Señor
Garcia—or Miguel, as she must now get used
to calling him—knew this person. The sensation of threat that had been present ever since
the stranger had spoken dissipated just a little,
too. Perhaps, being so impressive in every de-
tectable department, this haughty creature
found it normal to look at lesser beings as if
they were beneath his lofty contempt.

Her mouth softening with relief at having
sorted out the less than flattering vibes
winging in her direction from what had to be

the most spectacularly handsome guy she'd ever seen, she moved closer to the old gentleman, as if for protection, as he proclaimed with enthusiasm, 'It's so good to see you—it's been a long time! How long are you staying in Cadiz?'

'Long enough to take you to lunch, Tio.' Long enough to warn him of the type of creature he had taken into his home, to redouble his efforts to persuade him to move into the family country home, or at the very least to move into his luxurious apartment here in Cadiz.

Studiously ignoring the new 'housekeeper', Cayo extended a lean, tanned hand. 'Shall we go?' To his amazed annoyance he received a decisive shake of his uncle's head. Until now Tio Miguel had always pandered to his every request or suggestion—except, of course, over the vexed question of his lifestyle.

'We shall lunch here,' Miguel stated with firm good humour. 'Izzy shall cook for us. We have pilchards, I'm told. And peaches.' He smiled down at her and laid a hand on her shoulder. 'Izzy, may I introduce my workaholic nephew, Cayo?'

His nephew! Not in the least impressed now, Izzy shot the poor old gentleman's uncaring relative a withering glance. If he could afford to dress himself in designer gear and sport a watch that must have cost thousands—and she knew about that sort of stuff because her brilliant, well-heeled big brother always dressed in the best, proclaiming that his position demanded it and that quality always counted— then surely he could alleviate his uncle's hand-to-mouth existence and visit more often to check on his welfare? As Miguel had said, it had been a long time.

Barely registering Cayo's response to the introduction, she drew herself up to her unspectacular height and stated, 'I'll start preparing lunch, Miguel.'

She headed for the kitchen, hoping the pilchards would stretch to feed three and not much caring for the idea of cooking for someone who had looked at her as if she were dirt. And how had he known her name? She should have asked—would have done if his chilling look hadn't frozen her vocal cords. It was an omission she would rectify over lunch. Unless he refused to share a table with a mere menial.

Watching her go through narrowed eyes, Cayo recalled how Augustin del Amo had described her. *A lush little package.* Very apt indeed.

The top of her silvery blond head might reach the top of his chest—or almost. And the descriptive 'lush' perfectly suited the ripe curves, full lips and eyes like bruised pansies. She found money an aphrodisiac and despite outward appearances she would know Miguel was rolling in the stuff. After all, she was already intimate enough to call Miguel by his given name!

Reining back the fiery impulse to go after her, take her by the scruff of her neck and tip her into the gutter where she clearly belonged, he turned to his uncle. 'I need to talk to you.'

* * *

The sight of the tiny kitchen, with its old-fashioned iron range, arrays of gleaming copper pans hanging from hooks on roughly plastered walls, earthenware platters and bowls perched on shelves, and the chunky wooden table that served as the only work surface always cheered Izzy, and today went some way to smooth her ruffled feathers.

Five weeks ago, when she'd walked in here for the first time to fetch the frail old gentleman a glass of water, she'd been horrified. Evidence of neglect had hit her from every side. Grease and dust had covered every surface, and the copper pans had been green with verdigris. Empty sherry bottles had been piled in one corner, and the heel of a mouldy loaf had rested in a bucket beneath the grimy stone sink.

'You live alone?' she'd asked as she'd watched him drink the water and set the mug aside, on top of a cluttered desk.

'Since my housekeeper left two days ago,' he supplied with a weak smile. 'I thought I should make myself something to eat, and I got the range going, but there was nothing to cook. I was on my way to market when I became light-headed. And I thank you,' he added with courtesy, 'for assisting me to my home.'

Definitely not ready to bow out with a *Think nothing of it*, Izzy asked, 'Do you have family I could contact for you?'

'Just a nephew, who I think at the moment is in Britain.' He spread his thin, fine-boned hands. 'In any case, it is not necessary to trouble anyone. Already I am recovered from my giddiness and feel better.'

He certainly didn't look it. Remembering that he'd been on his way to market to buy food, she asked, 'When did you last eat?'

'I don't recall.' He looked as if the question really puzzled him, and explained earnestly, with a frail hand indicating the mass of books and papers on the desk, 'When I'm working I forget time.'

'Then how about I save you the trouble and

pop out for some food?' Izzy was back on her tortured feet, not prepared to leave this poor old man to his own ineffectual devices—at least not until he'd been fed and persuaded to give her the name and address of his doctor.

Heading for the nearest shop, she had found her outraged thoughts kept her from dwelling on her burningly painful feet. Deserted by a housekeeper who, from what she'd seen, hadn't been too keen on doing any work, with his only relative obviously not keeping in touch because the old gentleman wasn't sure where he was. She was already feeling anxious and even slightly cross on his behalf.

Raiding her precious euros, she bought eggs, oil and crusty rolls and tottered back. Half an hour later, watching the colour return to his ashen cheeks as he ate the scrambled eggs and one of the rolls, she chatted away. She was concerned that he absolutely refused to see his doctor, but happy to answer his questions because his curiosity must surely mean he was feeling more himself. So she told him exactly how she'd landed up in Spain, and regaled him with her family history. She glossed over the humiliation she'd suffered at Marcus's hands, and when she came to her present unenviable jobless and homeless situation she gave the half-truth that being a mother's help hadn't suited.

'So what will you do now?' Miguel asked.

Izzy twisted her hands together in her lap, her huge eyes clouding. Since helping the old gentleman to his feet she'd actually forgotten her own misery. Deflatedly, she confessed, 'I don't know. I hoped I would find something here in Cadiz to tide me over. But so far—nothing.'

'Couldn't your parents help?'

Izzy shuddered. And then, because his interest was obviously kindly, she admitted, 'They could—and they would. But I can't face telling them I've failed again. When I left school my dad—like I told you, he was a solicitor—sort of made a job for me in his practice. Being senior partner, he swung it.

Then when he retired my parents went out to New Zealand to be with James—my brother. They wanted me to go with them but I wouldn't,' she confided earnestly.

She was relieved to be unburdening herself because usually her family and the people she worked with didn't think she had anything worth listening to, and this old gentleman was hanging on every word she said.

'James is so clever, you see. He sailed through every exam he ever took, and now he's a highly regarded surgeon. My parents are hugely proud of him, of course. Not being anything special, *I've* always been a disappointment to them. To make it worse James married a brainy woman— a top lawyer. Being around them always makes me feel squashed. So I stayed back in England. They weren't at all pleased when I gave up my job in the practice and came to Spain. So I want to get back on my feet by my own efforts and not go crawling to them for help.'

He nodded understandingly and asked, 'And

you left your work in England because you had
a falling-out with a young man? From what
you told me earlier you were very fond of him.
If you returned to England do you think you
could patch things up?'

Izzy went bright pink. She'd been so humili-
ated she didn't like to think about it. But maybe
she should get it out of her system—and it was
certainly much easier to talk to a stranger.

'It wasn't like that.' She sighed. 'I feel a real
fool. But I had this huge crush on him—
Marcus. He's a legal executive in Dad's old
practice, really good-looking—good at
making a girl feel special. I thought we were
close, you know. He asked me to do little
things for him—stuff like collecting his dry
cleaning in my lunch hour, doing bits of
shopping. He took me out once, and bought
me a glass of wine. That's when he told me his
housekeeper had thrown a wobbly and walked
out and left him without a cleaner. When I vol-
unteered to help him out he called me his

treasure and held my hand. Said I was special. He made me feel valued for a change. How stupid can a girl get?'

Surreptitiously she eased her shoes off and allowed her agonised toes the freedom to curl with embarrassment. Then she took a deep breath and confided, 'I heard him talking to Molly, one of the secretaries, obviously responding to something she'd said. "Sure, she can't take those big googly eyes off me—but long live the crush if it means I get a free errand girl, laundry service and cleaner! All I have to do is turn on the charm, call her my treasure and she'll walk backwards over hot coals for me!" And Molly just laughed and said, "Not in those scary high heels she wears, she won't!" I felt like the world's biggest idiot.'

His weary eyes on her flushed, embarrassed features, Miguel Garcia said, 'So you need work and I, it would appear, need a housekeeper. The position's yours if you want it—until you get back on your feet. There will be a weekly house-keeping allowance, and you will receive the same wage as Benita did.' He named a sum that was slightly less than the pittance the del Amos had paid her, but beggars couldn't be choosers, and if she was really careful she could save enough over time to fund a transfer to another destination.

In the meantime she could sort the poor old gentleman out, make sure he ate regularly and that his home was clean, and later contact the Spanish equivalent of the British Social Services to keep an eye on him after she'd left.

'Thanks!' she beamed. 'I'd love to work for you!'

And she was loving it, Izzy thought now as she reached for a heavy-bottomed copper pan and the olive oil. Already she was fond of her poor old gentleman, as she always thought of him. The owner of a soft heart, she'd always been on the side of the underdog, and seeing her employer grow stronger and sprightlier every day was, to her, better than winning the Lottery.

'I don't believe a word of it!' Miguel stated with cold fury. 'Izzy is no more an immoral gold-digger than I am! And if you mix with the type of person who would stoop to spread such a calumny then I am disappointed in you.'

'Of necessity, Tio.' Cayo received the reprimand with a slight upward shift of one wide shoulder. 'Augustin del Amo is a highly respected banker. I occasionally do business with him.' Unsurprised by his uncle's defence of Miss Sweetness and Light—as the older man innocently claimed her to be—Cayo leaned back in the chair on the other side of the cluttered desk, the tips of his steepled fingers resting against the hard line of his mouth.

Izzy Makepeace was smart. Smart enough to know she had to tread carefully. Because the stakes were higher this time. She wasn't angling to be a wealthy married man's paid mistress but something else entirely. An indispensable treasure, caring for an even wealthier man as his age advanced. A wife!

The thought made his blood run cold! No way would he stand by and see his beloved, innocently naïve relative walk into *that* trap!

'How much do you pay her?' he asked with deceptive smoothness. Receiving the information that she earned the same as Benita had done, he dipped his dark head in understanding.

As long as the unlamented Benita had had enough to buy cheap sherry and didn't have to exert herself by so much as an extra intake of breath in the non-commission of her duties she would have been happy enough to receive wages that hadn't increased in the last twenty years. Even she would have known that her so-called services weren't worth any more, and his uncle, unaware of the cost of living because he lived firmly in the past, in the company of long-dead saints, and rarely read a newspaper or listened to a radio, wouldn't know he was paying what amounted to peanuts. He would have been horrified if the fact had been pointed out to him.

But no sane young working woman would accept such low payment. Not unless she had an ulterior motive. If he'd had doubts before—and he hadn't—that would have clinched it. She had her motive!

'Do you realise that what you're paying her is a fraction of the going rate?' Seeing his uncle's brows draw together, Cayo pressed on with barely concealed exasperation. 'Of course you don't. You don't live in the real world—never have done. Since leaving the university where you taught medieval history twenty years ago you've buried yourself in research. You have no idea what goes on in the world. So why would a young healthy woman accept such low pay? Think about it.'

Leaving the older man looking every one of his seventy-six years and more, Cayo strode from the study and flung open the door to the kitchen.

He had to admit that the room had scrubbed up well. But then it would be in her best interests to work her socks off, present herself as an angel of mercy, indispensable, when the glittering prize was a pot of gold at the end of the rainbow, he rationalised with an ingrained cynicism born of having to fight off greedy little gold-diggers ever since he'd reached his late teens.

She had her back to him, was removing a heavy pan from the stove with both hands.

'I'm just about to dish up, Miguel. If you and your nephew would go up to the dining room I'll be with you in a tick.'

Her cheerful words set his teeth on edge.

She turned then, her smile fading fast when she saw him. He noted the way she banged the pan down on the tabletop and hauled her shoulders back, her eyes very bright.

'Right, mister!' she spluttered. 'I've got something to say to you—'

He cut across her, having no interest in

hearing anything from her beyond a meekly compliant goodbye.

'How much will it take to make yourself scarce, be out of this house before nightfall and never come near my uncle again?' Cayo demanded, gazing steadily at her, his black-as-midnight eyes as cold as charity, his feet planted firmly apart, his fists pushed into the pockets of his chinos. 'Name your price.'

CHAPTER THREE

'WHAT did you say?'

Momentarily stunned, Izzy released a disbelieving gasp. She planted her hands on the table, leaning forward, and searched his dark eyes for any sign that he could be joking. Finding none, she added at full outraged volume, 'You're offering me money to walk out of my job and leave Miguel in the lurch? I don't believe this!' She huffed out a breath and imparted, 'I'll have you know he's as good at looking after himself as a two-year-old.' Then, introducing a note of scorn, 'You wouldn't know, of course, because it seems you're rarely around, but your uncle collapsed in the street. It took me three weeks to persuade him to go for a check-up, He's got a heart murmur, not helped by borderline malnutrition, so you're off your rocker if you think I'd leave him to fend for himself for a pocketful of euros! What sort of nephew are you?'

'One who wasn't born yesterday.'

Smooth as silk, he slid into the rough grit of her attack. Stopped in her tracks by that weird statement, Izzy connected with the silver gleam of cynicism in those compelling eyes.

She suppressed a sudden unwelcome shiver as he added, almost purring, 'You have a saying, I believe? A bird in the hand is worth two in the bush. So, I say again, name your price.'

She tossed her silvery blond head high, and her normally water-clear blue eyes were shadowed by a bewildered frown as she demanded tersely, 'Why?'

'Because I know your sort,' Cayo supplied drily. 'And I have confirmation via Augustin del Amo. Remember him?' His own arrogantly held head was high, too. Brilliant eyes narrowed, he reminded her with harsh conviction, 'Instead of looking after his children as you were paid to—highly paid, by all accounts—you spent all your time trying to tempt him into changing your job description to that of paid and pampered mistress.'

Her stomach swooping, looping and finally knotting, her cheeks flaming, Izzy gulped back a yelp of outrage and finally vented, 'That creep!'

Señora del Amo had promised her name would be mud! And she hadn't wasted any time spreading the lies she'd chosen to believe rather than accept that her husband was a real slimeball. She could just about understand that. But this horrible man—neglecter of frail, impoverished old uncles—was choosing to believe the worst of her without doing her the courtesy of asking to hear her side of the story!

As if that wasn't enough, worse was to come. He pointed out with icy cool, 'Get it into your mercenary little head that there's nothing here for you. You may be able to fool an unworldly old man, but you don't fool me. Take cash in hand and leave—or I'll make sure you regret the day you were born.'

He was a maniac! Izzy decided, feeling as if she'd landed in a parallel universe. Okay, so he'd taken the wealthy banker's words at face value and decided she was a mercenary little scrubber, out for all she could get from the male of the species. So why tell her there was nothing for her here, when anyone could see that Miguel barely had two pennies to rub together?

This man might be prime contender in a competition to find the world's most gorgeous male, but the handsome exterior clothed a nasty mind, she decided, straightening her spine. She wasn't going to even begin to plead her case, because she'd be wasting her breath, nor go on to explain that she already got plenty out of working for Miguel. Like making his living conditions more comfortable, seeing his health improve.

She'd leave only when she was sure outside help was forthcoming. So this handsome devil could take his threats and swallow them. And she hoped they choked him!

A saccharine smile hiding her internal boiling fury, she forced herself to unclench her small fists and slid the fish onto the waiting platter. 'Take this up while I tell Miguel lunch is ready,' she instructed snippily. 'And since you ask me to name my price for making myself scarce, then try this for size.' She squared her narrow shoulders and gave him exactly what he deserved. 'Ten billion. Pounds sterling. In cash. All neat and tidy in a gigantic diamond-studded gold crate. And while we're at it, a nice villa in the hills to put it in!'

Mentally adding, *So put that in your pipe and smoke it, señor!* she made a speedy exit.

Lunch was a dismal affair. Izzy was too angry to eat more than a mouthful and Miguel, usually so talkative even if the subject matter was so rarefied it went straight over her head, was preoccupied, barely uttering a word. She had the horrible feeling that Cayo had poured his poison into his elderly relative's ears and that—even worse—the poor old gentleman had believed him!

Only Cayo seemed at ease. The only sign of his deeply unflattering opinion of her, and his stated intent to make her regret the day she'd been born if she didn't do as he'd ordered, was the slight twisting of his sexy mouth whenever she tried to break the uncomfortable silence with some admittedly inane comment or other.

And then he put down his fruit knife, wiped fastidious fingers on one of the fine linen napkins she'd discovered at the bottom of a drawer and carefully laundered, leaned back in his chair and drawled, 'I hear, Tio, that you are unwell?' He raised an imperious silencing hand as Miguel, startled back into the here and now by that unwelcome reminder, opened his mouth to deny any such thing. 'I intend to get all the facts from your doctor this afternoon. So any blustering denials you are preparing will be neither here nor there.'

Catching sight of Miguel's quizzical glance, one brow raised in her direction above deep-set dark eyes, Izzy pinkened and confessed, 'I thought I should mention it.' She aimed an accusing stare at Cayo's tough expression. 'After all, you've been neglected for too long. Someone should take care of you and make sure you eat and rest properly.'

'Something you do to perfection.'

The gentleness of her employer's tone, the warmth of his smile made Izzy feel faint with relief. If his nephew *had* relayed the del Amos' lies then he clearly hadn't believed them.

She would have felt wretched if he had. She had grown fond of her old gentleman, impractical dreamer that he was; looking after him was like looking after an extra clever elderly babe in arms, and this time she hadn't failed— in fact she'd made a success of her current job.

That empowering thought gave her the confidence to stand up from the table and address the brute sitting opposite. 'I insist Miguel rests for an hour in the afternoon. Thank you for dropping by. I'll see you out.'

The older man's low, delighted chuckle had brought a dark, angry flush to his nephew's fiercely handsome features, Izzy noted with immense satisfaction as he got to his feet, towering over her. Neatly sidestepping him, she led the way down the dingy staircase and through a narrow door that led into the tiny cobbled courtyard she longed to brighten with tubs of flowers. But she knew such a luxury was out of the question when money was so obviously tight. Which glaring fact gave her the resolution to turn and face the man as she reached the street door.

My, he was tall! Wishing she had the advantage of a pair of her highest high heels, now stowed away in the bottom of a cupboard in her small bedroom, she tipped back her head to meet his lethally contemptuous black eyes. She absolutely refused to let herself be intimidated by those powerfully muscled shoulders and chest, or wonder why the eye contact took her breath away and sent a frisson of unwelcome physical awareness shooting deep into her pelvis.

'You obviously believe the worst of everyone,' she stated, doing her best to get her breathing back on an even keel. 'But ask yourself this—if I'm a greedy little scrubber, out for all I can get, why would I be wasting my time here with a man who's as poor as a church mouse? What do you think I'm going to do? Steal his spoons? And, while we're on the subject, you offered me money to make myself scarce, so you've obviously got some to spare. I suggest you use it to give your uncle an allowance—enough to make his existence a little less hand-to-mouth.'

In receipt of his abrupt, tight-lipped, non-verbal departure, Izzy banged the street door shut behind him and jumped up and down, hugging herself. She'd sent him packing with a flea in his ear! She couldn't remember when she'd last felt so alive!

The arrogant so-and-so had walked in, looking oh-so superior, and tried to make her leave because he believed lies. Naturally his sort would take the word of a wealthy banker over any denial that might come from a mere menial!

But she had refused to go. Just thinking of the utterly ridiculous payment she had demanded made her giggle. And—the icing on the cake—she had lectured him about his neglect of his uncle. With a bit of luck his conscience, if he had one—which was debatable, she conceded—just might move him in the direction of helping the poor old gentleman financially.

She had won the battle!

The fight was well and truly on, Cayo thought grimly as he left the doctor's office, crossed Calle San Francisco Nueva and headed through the maze of narrow streets back towards Miguel's humble dwelling. On two fronts.

Izzy Makepeace might think she was clever, pretending she was unaware that Miguel was an extremely wealthy man, but it was common knowledge that the absent-minded scholar was loaded. He had no interest in material comforts or possessions, and lived only for his painstaking work—information that would have been easy to pick up working for Señora del Amo, who was a notorious gossip and claimed to know everyone who was anyone and exactly what they were worth. A wealthy eccentric, a descendant of one of Spain's oldest and most respected families, would certainly be worth talking about—even boasting, perhaps, of the business connection.

When Isabel Makepeace had failed to establish herself as a wealthy banker's mistress she would have hung around the Topete area, where Miguel had his home. No believer in coincidence, he knew she must have planned on doing her best to get to meet the man she knew as a better-than-well-heeled elderly bachelor, grasping her opportunity when the poor old guy had collapsed virtually under her nose.

That she fully intended to get her claws into his naïve uncle and not let go had been proved a rock-solid fact when she'd answered his invitation to name her price with that ludicrously greedy demand.

She was after a lifetime of financial security. Make herself indispensable, Miss Sweetness and Light, then wheedle an offer of marriage from the wealthy old man and embark on the sort of high living that would leave his uncle floundering and hurt. He could think of no other reason for a mercenary harpie to work so hard for a pittance—and the evidence of the much improved state of his uncle's home suggested that she did work hard.

His jaw hardened with steely determination. Tio Miguel could be exasperating, but he loved him. Far too much to stand by and see that scheming, greedy little blond pocket Venus ruin the years remaining to him and make him a laughing stock. He, Cayo Angel Garcia, would *not* stand by and see that happen.

And the news from Miguel's doctor had been a wake-up call. The heart murmur of itself wasn't too serious. But coupled with his neglected physical condition…

Guilt scored a line between winging black brows. True, he had lost count of the times he'd tried to persuade the elderly man to make his home at the *castillo*, where he could be well looked after. But after continuous polite refusal to take advantage of his nephew's hospitality or to dismiss Benita, who'd been with him for years, Cayo had backed off, believing that every man had the right to live his life as he felt fit.

A mistake he deeply regretted.

One that wouldn't be repeated. Liberal tolerance was now a thing of the past where his uncle's wellbeing was concerned.

'You work too hard,' Miguel chided gently, finding Izzy in the kitchen ironing his shirts after rising from his siesta. 'And, as Cayo pointed out, I pay you far too little.' He shook his grey head, annoyed with himself. 'I was unaware. I should think of things outside my narrow field of interest. I apologise. Cayo can be shortsighted and stubborn in some respects, I fear, but in this instance he is right. You must allow me to make amends. Will you tell me how excellent housekeepers *should* be financially rewarded? And by the same token tell me the modern-day cost of keeping a modest household such as ours running?'

Her soft mouth open, Izzy stared at her employer in shock. Not because he'd actually woken up to the fact that the cost of living had risen in the last twenty or so years, but because his brute of a nephew had actually pointed it out.

If he was so keen to rid his uncle of her contaminating presence, why had he asked what she was earning and given his opinion that it was far too little?

Unless, of course—her smooth brow furrowed—the information gained from his uncle had cemented his distrust of her into rock-hard certainty. He thought she was working for next to nothing because she had some ulterior motive, had something to gain. But what?

'Well?' Miguel broke gently into her puzzled train of thought just as Cayo sauntered into the room, giving her no time to assemble her wits and make a reply, or give her old gentleman information that would make him feel really uncomfortable and put him in a spot—because it was obvious that he wouldn't be able to pay the going rate.

Suddenly the room seemed airless. Cayo's formidable presence dominated the space with the unmistakable aura of the alpha male—born to lead, to take on all comers without batting an eyelid. For some unknown reason it made her feel decidedly dizzy, and she felt herself flush with some strange emotion she couldn't put a name to. She turned away to take another shirt from the laundry basket, with the image of the way he looked—six foot plus of prime Spanish manhood, from the commanding width of his shoulders tapering down to a narrow waist, slinky hips and impressively long, elegantly trousered legs—indelibly printed on her retina.

'I have spoken at length with Dr Menendez, who gave me the results of the tests you underwent, Tio,' he announced, his tone so authoritative she could have smacked him.

Wandering farther into the room, he absorbed the cosy domestic scene. Miguel in the battered old armchair that had stood just inside the door for as long as he could remember, watching the Angel of Mercy ironing his shirts.

She was working to a different agenda from the one she had employed with Augustin del Amo, for sure. A real Miss Goody-Two-Shoes—caring and competent, catering to an elderly man's domestic comforts, delectable, with enticing strands of the spun-silver-gilt hair escaping the ribbon arrangement she'd pinned it back with. Her luscious curves were clad in a bog-standard T-shirt and cotton skirt, not overtly flaunting her steamy sexuality as her clothes would have done when she'd attempted to snare a rich banker, because those tactics wouldn't work with the elderly scholar.

Clever.

But he was smarter. By a cartload he was smarter!

Kill two birds with one stone. First get Tio Miguel to agree to move to the luxurious Castillo de las Palomas, where he could continue his work and be looked after by attentive staff who would cater to his every need. Cayo would suggest he took his housekeeper with him as companion because, judging by what he'd seen and heard, his uncle was already fond of the little tramp. He felt comfortable with her, and in all likelihood would dig his heels in and refuse to go anywhere if it meant his housekeeper was to be cast out on the street.

Then he would seduce Izzy Makepeace away from her intention to get her claws into the older man—no hardship, because the sultry, passionate fullness of her lips belied the wide, childlike innocence of those big blue eyes, and he had never suffered difficulties in that direction. Quite the opposite. The ease with which he seemed to attract simpering females anxious to do anything to please him had bored him since his hormones had run riot in his teens.

He would seduce her, make sure his uncle knew what was happening, and then make sure she was well and truly finished with.

His mouth tightened. He didn't like it. It felt uncomfortably like cruelty, and he had always prided himself on being straightforward in both personal and business dealings. But if he had to fight dirty he would. For his uncle's sake, he would.

Swinging round to face them, he stated, 'In view of what I learned from Menendez, I have a proposition to make.'

CHAPTER FOUR

Izzy folded the last of the shirts as a fierce stab of anxiety skittered its way through her entire body. This darkly handsome thorough-bred male looked as out of place in these shabby surroundings as a brilliant-cut diamond in a sack of potatoes. She was sure that whatever he proposed would bode no good for her. Cayo wanted her out of his uncle's home, and he didn't look the kind of guy who would give up easily.

'Tio—' Half sitting on the chunky table, he was addressing his relative.

Izzy, her ears tingling for the expected list of her supposed and damning sins, embellished with a strongly voiced suggestion that she be thrown back on the street where she belonged, permitted herself a tiny sigh of relief when he said gently, 'Menendez tells me that your heart problem was occasioned by the rheumatic fever you had as a child. At the time, apparently, the condition went unrecognised. You can live with it, he assures me, provided you take care. Something you haven't done for years—'

'Ah, but things have changed,' Miguel interrupted smartly. 'Unlike poor old Benita, whose sins of omission escaped me, Izzy makes sure I am looked after splendidly! Provided she agrees to stay on—at an increased rate of payment—we will be very comfortable together. You mustn't worry.'

'But I do,' Cayo countered firmly. 'Have done for years. You are of my family—blood of my blood. I care about you and I worry,' he incised, with a telling movement of one lean, bronzed hand. 'I have asked before—not with as much vigour as I should have done, perhaps—and this time I will insist. You must move to the cooler air of the mountains, at least during the debilitating heat of the summer. And who knows? You might be sensible enough to make it your permanent home. At the Castillo de las Palomas you will enjoy every comfort and luxury. As you well know, there are willing staff to cater to your every need. And there is also an excellent library, so you may continue your work, if you wish, in guaranteed privacy and peace. As far as I can see there is nothing, apart from your pigheadedness, to stop you behaving sensibly and in your own best interests.'

Grateful for the absence—so far—of the verbal assault she'd been expecting, and amazed that her slating opinion had actually moved Cayo to doing something about his uncle's wellbeing, Izzy held her breath.

She was unprepared for the elderly man's stubbornness. Despite being obviously touched by his nephew's offer, evidenced by the sudden moistness of his dark eyes, he declined. 'I'm grateful for your concern, Cayo. Truly. But we are comfortable here, and you know how I dislike any kind of upheaval.'

Emboldened by the look Cayo turned to give her—his brows lifting in obvious frustration, his smile wry, as if they were on the same side for once—Izzy put in, 'Can I say something? It sounds just what the doctor ordered, Miguel—honestly.'

Feeling Cayo's gaze upon her, she met the flash of a very definite query in his spectacularly eloquent eyes and ignored it. That she would be jobless and homeless again didn't count against the old gentleman being properly looked after. She'd manage somehow. Miguel would have no need of a housekeeper—not with Cayo's 'willing staff'—and if his uncle could be persuaded to make the move he would have won, got rid of her supposedly poisonous presence without the outlay of a single euro of the bribe he'd so insultingly offered her.

The thought of him winning made her want to stamp her feet and scream! Yet despite that she knew that urging Miguel to accept the offer was the right thing to do.

She'd risen to the challenge of her present job—warmed to the concept of being a real help, useful and valued for once in her life—but she'd always meant to leave when she was satisfied that her old gentleman would be looked after and not left alone to his own absent-minded devices.

She was stunned when the man who had vowed to make her regret the day she was born now imparted, with the silken confidence of one who knew a weak spot when he saw one and had no hesitation in going straight for it, 'I know you better than you realise, Tio. In the past you have always refused my repeated offers because you have a kind heart—one of the gentlest and kindest, I know. To have availed yourself of comfortable surroundings and the best care would have meant dismissing Benita. So I suggest—urge—that you now bring Izzy with you, as your paid companion.'

Stunned by his suggestion, Izzy was left breathless when he turned again to her and gave her a smile of such dazzling brilliance that she came over all feverish. She could hardly believe what she was hearing as he continued, 'That way you won't be throwing her out of work and making her homeless, so your conscience won't give you indigestion! And I will be more than happy to welcome her as a guest in my home.'

Her mouth made an O of sheer astonishment as she stared at his dark, strong and shatteringly sexy features, searching for clues to his totally out-of-character behaviour. Her jumbled brain cells barely registered Miguel's amused reply. 'In that case, I agree. My hardworking house-keeper deserves a summer break after all her kindness to a foolish old man.'

She only scrambled for her senses after Cayo's elegantly long legs had carried him to the door, with the information that he was heading back to his apartment to await an expected fax from Hong Kong, but would be in touch later to make the necessary arrangements for their removal to his mountain home.

Closing her still gaping mouth, she watched him leave. He was up to something. Something devious. And that was scary. He'd offered her money to leave, called her names, and made it plain that he thought her a species of low-life—and yet here he was, actually smiling at her, saying he'd welcome her as a guest in his no-doubt palatial home. A castle, no less. It made no sense at all.

'You've made the right decision,' she told the older man. 'From what your nephew said it sounds as if you'll have every comfort and care, and he seems genuinely fond of you.' She conceded this somewhat unwillingly, because she didn't want to admit there was anything remotely human or caring about the guy—at least where she was concerned. 'He'll be glad to provide for you,' she went on, 'but count me out. I can't go with you. You won't need a housekeeper. I'd only be a freeloader. I'd rather earn an honest crust, and I'll soon find another job, you'll see,' she ended, hoping she sounded more confident than she felt.

'I understand,' Miguel responded flatly. 'But if that's your decision I won't go either. We'll carry on as we are.' His angular face softened in a smile. 'In fact, now I come to think of it, I'm perfectly happy where I am.'

The penny dropped. Cayo must have foreseen this, she realised sinkingly. After all, he had to know his relative far better than she did. Hadn't he intimated that the only reason the old gentleman hadn't taken up his offer before had been because his uncle's tender conscience wouldn't have been easy if he'd made his previous housekeeper unemployed? Probably unemployable, judging by the state his humble little home had been in when Izzy had first set eyes on it.

In all probability Miguel would have confided in his nephew—told him of her own sorry circumstances when they'd first met—leading the younger man to realise that, having taken in a waif and stray, his gentle, soft-hearted uncle wasn't about to throw her out on the street!

Hence the amazing suggestion that she tag along, too, until he thought up some spectacularly nasty way to get rid of her! It made perfect sense.

Nothing else for it in the circumstances. But she was confident that once her old gentleman got settled in comfortable surroundings, with three good meals a day produced like clock-work, and no more scrimping and scraping, he would accept a sudden bout of homesickness, or a fictitious job offer back in her own country. Her decision to leave would be made before Cayo had worked out how to get her thrown out of his aristocratic home and probably out of the country. So, ignoring her better judgement, she told him breezily, 'If you insist on being stubborn then, okay—I'll go along, too. I've never lived in a castle before—should be fun. When do we go? Did he say?'

* * *

The opulent chauffeur-driven car took the steep gradients with effortless ease and, having finally overcome her fear of the hairpin bends and terrifying sheer drops, Izzy began to relax and enjoy the ever-changing vista. Precipitous mountains dropped to deep river valleys hazed over with the silvery green of olive groves and the deeper green of forest trees, occasionally broken by the clustered rooftops of picturesque villages.

She would relax and go with the flow, she decided. Something she was good at, apparently. Her full lips curved into an amused smile as she recalled one of many lectures delivered by her father. 'Unlike James, you have no direction! You meander through life, drifting from one dead-end job to another—have you no ambition?'

Not of the academic kind. There was no way she could compete with her older, cleverer, much praised and doted-upon brother, so she didn't even try.

What her parents had never understood was

that she *did* have an ambition. To fall in love, marry the man she loved, create a home together filled with warmth and love, and have children together. Children who would be equally adored and cherished, regardless of talent or lack thereof.

So far it was an unfulfilled ambition. The boys she'd dated in her teens had only been interested in one thing. Suspecting that because of her generous curves, and what James had once scathingly described as her 'blond bimbo looks', they'd clearly thought she would have been easy to get into bed and she'd steered clear, and put her secret ambition on hold until she'd met Marcus. She'd believed he was the one—that he really liked her, valued her. And he'd never tried to get her into the bedroom, which surely had to mean he'd respected her? In her mind's eye she had pictured his tall blond figure waiting as she floated up the aisle.

Alarmingly, the remembered and now despised image faded, and a tall dark figure, stiff with Spanish pride, took its place. Izzy gulped, and blinked the fleeting mind picture away with extreme violence.

To add to her discomfiture, Miguel said from beside her, in an excruciatingly embarrassing coincidence, 'My nephew really should cease his unemotional, businesslike arrangements with his occasional mistresses and take a wife. Las Palomas is exquisite, but sterile in its beauty. It needs a family to bring it to life. He will be there, waiting for us, and I shall tell him so. When the time is right.' He chuckled, as if something had amused him.

Too mortified by the mental image her subconscious had thrown up to respond directly, she asked instead, just to change the subject, 'You are familiar with his castle?'

'I was born there,' was his lightly dismissive response. 'It has been in our family for many generations. I left to attend university in England, and after gaining my doctorate I lectured. America, mainly. I rarely visited my family, and after the deaths of my parents—one shortly following the other, sadly—I never went again. Roman, my brother who was Cayo's father, had the use of Las Palomas while I preferred to live the quiet life of a humble scholar. The family have great wealth—'

'Let me get this straight,' Izzy butted in, wriggling round in her seat to face him more squarely, her brow pleated as she tried to follow what he was saying. Her voice was sharp with outrage on her old gentleman's behalf. 'You mean your brother got the lot—wealth and the castle and everything—and you got nothing?'

'Good heavens, child! What gave you that idea? As the oldest son I inherited vast landed estates, while Roman took over the shipping business—which I believe Cayo has expanded massively since his father passed away. He also finds time to manage the income from my estates—investments and suchlike. I have never been interested in the acquisition of material wealth. I have annual meetings with Cayo and his money men, and although I am grateful for my nephew's husbandry I must admit I find it all tedious. In any case,' he added more cheerfully, 'all I own will pass to Cayo in time, which is as it should be. The Garcia estates, properties and businesses will be under one ownership again, not divided.'

Her ready tongue stilled by Miguel's disclosure, Izzy struggled to get her thoughts in order. She ignored her companion's comments on the landmarks they were passing with aristocratic stateliness.

Despite all appearances the elderly man wasn't dirt-poor, struggling to exist on a pittance. He had to be loaded!

For the first time since she had known him she wanted to shake him! So, okay, he wasn't interested in money—given his other-worldliness, she could go along with that—but the thought of the way she'd boasted about her canniness in going to the market minutes before it closed to

take advantage of stallholders who were virtually giving produce away made her feel such a
fool. He might have taken the opportunity—
and there had been many—to tell her that such
frugality wasn't necessary, or at least to enquire
if the housekeeping allowance was so inadequate that it required such desperate measures.

She could forgive all that—laugh about it,
even—but the misunderstanding had had dire
consequences.

Cayo had believed those lies. Izzy
Makepeace had been thrown out on her ear
because she'd been trying to seduce a re-
spectable banker and ensconce herself as his
paid mistress, and next he'd heard she'd turned
up as his wealthy uncle's housekeeper.

Up to no good.

An impression she must have confirmed with
her demand for billions of pounds! Letting him
think that a mere pay-off wouldn't satisfy her—
that she was intent on getting her hands on his
uncle's fortune!

Apart from being fond of his elderly relative, and not wanting to see him falling into the clutches of a woman he saw as a mercenary gold-digger, he wouldn't want to lose his inheritance.

Enough motive to explain his chilling threat that he'd make her regret the day she'd been born if she didn't remove herself from his uncle's vicinity. It came back to haunt her. He'd meant it! She was going to have to confront him with the facts—make him understand that she had believed all along that his eccentric uncle had nothing more substantial to live on than some measly pension or other. It was imperative she make him believe that in agreeing to work for the old gentleman she hadn't had designs on a fortune she hadn't even known existed.

'We are arriving.'

The volume at which Miguel's statement was delivered alerted her to the possibility that it wasn't the first time he'd given that snippet of information. Izzy blinked and refocused her eyes. A high stone wall snaked down the mountainside, and they were entering a curving driveway that wound its way to a magnificent fortified palace—a statement of power and wealth if ever she saw one. Her stomach wriggled with a flock of hyperactive butterflies.

How was she going to convince the cynical owner of this lot that she was innocent of all accusations? Convince him so thoroughly that he'd rethink whatever devious plans he'd made in order to carry out his earlier threat when she'd already dug her grave with her too-ready tongue?

CHAPTER FIVE

As THE stately car passed through a massive stone arch and drew to a well-bred halt in the inner courtyard, Cayo got to his feet and left the arbour-shaded carved stone bench, emerging into dazzling sunlight.

Phase one completed. The grim line of his mouth softened. His beloved mule-headed uncle was finally safely back where he belonged, to be surrounded by the comfort and luxury that was his birthright. His conscience could rest easily in that respect.

Phase two was yet to be started. The successful removal of one money-grabbing blonde. His thickly fringed dark eyes sharpened with steely intent, boding ill for anyone with the temerity to cross him.

Advancing, he forced a welcoming smile and watched his chauffeur step round to open a rear door. He handed the little gold-digger out before moving round to perform the same courtesy for his uncle.

Waiting in cynical expectation for her to trip eagerly to Miguel's side, tuck her arm solicitously through his and simper up at him from her diminutive height, Cayo narrowed his eyes as instead of acting out the part he'd mentally assigned her she made a beeline across the courtyard to where he was standing.

Her silvery blond hair was, as usual, artfully tousled in a naturally sexy style that many women would gladly pay top dollar to achieve. She was dressed in a faded top that lovingly cleaved to her bountiful breasts, and cotton trousers that tantalisingly moulded her thighs and ended just below her knees. As his body reacted in a despised surge of lust, he wondered, at a tangent, how such bog-standard clothes could make her look so provocatively sensual, when the groomed and expertly painted women who circled like hopeful sharks on the periphery of his life could spend thousands on designer exclusives and leave his libido stone-cold.

He shouldn't knock his primitive response to what Augustin del Amo had lip-lickingly described as 'a lush little package', he supposed acidly, given the task ahead of him.

She had refused to accept a financial inducement to leave his uncle alone, therefore it was up to him to seduce her away from any thought of getting her claws into the older man. A task that sat ill with his ingrained sense of chivalry and honour, honed by centuries of ancestral Spanish pride.

He kept his smile in place with difficulty, hiding the grim, distasteful thoughts that occupied his mind as she pattered up to him. Her delicate cheekbones flushed a soft rose colour as she came to a halt and planted her hands on her curvaceous hips, and her neat chin tilted upwards as she demanded breathily, 'I need to talk to you. Now. In private.'

The smile vanished. His black eyes were cool and distant. She was in no position to make demands of him. 'If you will excuse me, it is my custom to see my guests settled.'

Ignoring her agitated, 'Oh—but listen—' he strode past her, and Izzy swung round to watch him greet his uncle, one arm around the older, shorter man's shoulders. For some reason she wished he could have greeted her that way, with obvious affection and warmth, and then she wished she hadn't wished that at all—because it showed her up as being really stupid.

And maybe she shouldn't have demanded they talk just like that, she decided, feeling flattened. He was obviously adding a total lack of manners to his tally of her sins, branding her as not fit for polite company. But she'd been so anxious to put him straight about her ignorance of Miguel's true financial situation that she had been able to think of nothing else, since the shattering revelation that, far from living a hand-to-mouth existence out of financial necessity, Miguel had no idea, and no interest in, how much he was worth.

Just like her to open her big mouth and put her foot in it!

Embarrassment painted her heart-shaped face with a hot flood of fiery colour as the two men joined her. Miguel flung an arm wide, encompassing the courtyard, the magnificent central fountain, the tubs of exotic flowering shrubs and the white doves fluttering from the shady stone arcades that led through to the no-doubt sumptuous living quarters, and asked, 'You approve, Izzy?'

'I'm sure your companion is most suitably impressed,' Cayo said drily, before she could respond, and immediately cursed himself for the sarcastic tone. He was going to have to try harder—to act in a duplicitous manner completely foreign to his straightforward nature if he was to have a hope in hell of persuading her that of the two vast fortunes she could see dangling in front of her greedy eyes *his* was the one to aim for.

'Ramona—my housekeeper—will show you to the rooms that have been readied for you, Tio,' Cayo imparted. Izzy trailed after them as they entered a vast marble-paved hall. 'They are on the ground floor, close to the library. You will have no need to use stairs or find your way about the warren of passages—unless you wish to reacquaint yourself with your childhood home.' His austere features softened in a smile that made him seem human and just impossibly handsome, Izzy thought, deploring the toe-curling effect it had on her as he went on, 'And don't worry. Your books and papers have not been unpacked. No one will touch or muddle them,' he assured the older man gently. 'You may arrange them in the library at your leisure.'

He really cared about his uncle, Izzy granted

as introductions were made to the housekeeper and a handful of wide-eyed maids. Cayo gave instructions in rapid Spanish which sent the super-efficient-looking housekeeper leading Miguel to an arched doorway at the far side of the great hall and the maids scurrying to do his bidding. He spoke and things happened.

He firmly believed that she was up to no good—had attached herself to his uncle for mercenary reasons—and he cared enough for the old gentleman to make sure she took herself off with her tail between her legs. Now that she knew that her impoverished and neglected old gentleman was nothing of the sort, she could understand where he was coming from. Especially since he'd heard the del Amos' lies.

She shivered, and nearly leapt out of her skin when he touched the bare flesh of her arm, making her feel as if she'd been prodded by an electrically charged pin. It fuzzed up her brain to such an extent that she couldn't take in what he was saying until the pressure of those lean bronzed fingers around her arm increased and he repeated, 'I will show you to your suite of rooms and see you settled.'

'What? Oh, right—' She attempted to claim back her arm, but the pressure of his fingers simply increased as he led her to an enormous stone staircase. Mounting it, she felt like a prisoner being led to a cell and her mouth went dry. She had to explain. Had to. But, remembering her earlier *faux-pas*, she knew she had to wait and not launch forth when members of his staff were criss-crossing the hall below, well within earshot.

Partway up the soaring staircase, a corridor led off to the right, dimly lit, its stone walls hung with ancient and probably priceless tapestries. Ahead, the corridor branched in three directions. The whole place was an intimidating mystery.

Izzy wished she'd never agreed to come here. She only had because she had thought then that it was the right thing to do for the sake of

Miguel and his future wellbeing, believing as she had that he was existing on a mere pittance and it was time that his selfish, wealthy nephew took care of him.

But it hadn't been necessary. Miguel, had he been so minded, could have lived in luxury. She knew that now. Too late.

A blinding flash of insight had her digging her heels into the cool marble flooring and accusing, 'As you're so fond of calling the shots, why didn't you just go ahead and arrange for your uncle to have a properly paid, decent housekeeper years ago? You pretend to care for him, so you could have done that. It took me, a total stranger, about ten minutes to realise he's so wrapped up in his work he can't be bothered about taking proper care of himself!'

She met his black gaze without flinching. She knew the answer—didn't she just! He'd only muscled into his relative's life now, taken over, because he believed—wrongly—that she was about to weasel her way into taking his inheritance. As if he weren't already eye-wateringly wealthy in his own right! Greedy, or what?

He lifted his proud head, centuries of Spanish high breeding carved into the unforgettably handsome features. 'You will moderate your tone and keep your skewed opinions to yourself while you are a guest in my home,' he advised, as smooth and cold as glass.

He did not take personal attacks—especially not from a mouthy little madam who was no better than she should be. Seducing her away from her plans to get the naïve Miguel firmly in her clutches, the devious but necessary assignment he'd set himself, suddenly felt too far beneath his honourable nature to be contemplated. There had to be another way.

Acidly polite, he stepped ahead and suggested, 'Perhaps we may proceed?'

Cringing at that put-down, Izzy followed, engulfed by frustration. He was really good at making out she was an ill-mannered boor—not fit to sully his splendid home, where he was insulated by fabulous wealth and had an army of servants to cater to his slightest whim. But then he was labouring under the misapprehension that she was some sleazy sort of career mistress—that, having failed with the oily banker, she'd set her sights on his uncle.

Time to set the record straight. Convince him that she wasn't what he thought she was. A huge smile wreathed her expressive features as she imagined his grovelling apology—which she would consider and finally accept with dignity, giving herself the high moral ground for once!

On that cheering thought she pattered on, catching up with him as he flung open a door and stepped just inside the threshold of the loveliest room she'd ever set eyes on.

'Wow!' Her big eyes widened. Acres of luxurious white carpet, panelled walls painted a delicate misty primrose-yellow, tall windows with gauzy white drapes, a group of three comfy chairs upholstered in yellow silk placed around a low coffee table, bowls of beautifully arranged roses to perfume the air, and what looked like a fully stocked drinks cabinet.

Cayo dug his hands into the pockets of stylish chinos and drawled, 'Your sitting room. The bedroom is through that door, with *en suite* bathroom, of course. I'll leave you to relax and will see you at dinner.'

Her own bathroom. Of course—what else? The urge to explore was almost overwhelming, but the imperative to put Cayo Garcia straight was stronger. Smartly stepping in front of him, she folded her arms across her slender middle, lifting her face to his. 'Hang on a tick. I have to say something. It's really important.'

'*Sí?*' Strongly marked brows drew together as his eyes met hers. So deep a blue, with the almost childlike clarity of innocence. Deeply misleading. He sucked in a sharp breath. She had an exquisite face. Taken individually, her features were not perfect, but they added up to an exquisitely fascinating whole, framed by wayward strands of silver-gilt that looked as soft as silk.

'Tis a Pity She's a Whore, he thought with mental dryness, then, inexplicably, felt his heart lurch with a spasm of sadness at the waste of all this luscious loveliness, packaging, as it did, a mercenary and immoral soul.

'Listen—' Izzy knew she sounded breathless. She was having difficulty stringing words together in her head, never mind getting them out of her mouth. It was the way he was looking at her that was so dreadfully unsettling. It made her tummy squirm, then tense, her mouth run dry.

'Well?' Cayo murmured without intonation, grimly amused as he pondered on what she was going to come up with—what was now so important. Something as twisted as her last outburst, at a guess.

Izzy just stared, moistening her dry lips with the tip of her tongue, fighting the awful dart of heat in the pit of her tummy that looking into his dark eyes always produced. Eyes as beautiful as his commanding masculine features…

Making a huge effort, she got out, 'I know what you think of me, and I don't blame you. I guess you'd always take the word of a big-wheel banker and his wife over a lowly domestic servant. But I promise you it wasn't like that. I'm sorry to have to say this about your friend, a man you obviously respect, but Señor del Amo was the one trying it on, not the other way around.'

Once she'd launched forth, the words just came tumbling out. 'And I had no idea that Miguel wasn't dirt-poor until he told me on the way here. Truly! He told me that he was born here, that the family wealth had been divided between him and your father. It was the first I knew of it—and you could have knocked me down with a feather!'

Nice try. But not nearly good enough. Cayo's eyes followed the movement as she brushed a silvery strand back from her forehead, pink with effort. His thick black lashes drifted down over sparkling jet eyes as he took in the taut expectancy of her voluptuous body. She was waiting for him to say he believed her, to treat her as if she was all sweetness and light, take the heat off and leave her free to wheedle her way even further into Miguel's affections. Did she think he'd been born yesterday?

'I see.' He was almost purring now. 'So let's recap.' His smile was devastatingly challenging. 'You took pity on a poor old man, and agreed to keep house for him for the sort of miserable wages that would have had any normal working girl heading for the hills, out of the goodness of your heart?'

Izzy shifted uncomfortably. From his point of view her decision would look suspect, she recognised sickly. It was up to her to make him understand. She squared her slim shoulders and said, with far more confidence than she felt, 'I was in a fix, and so was he. He needed someone to keep house. I needed a job and a roof over my head. And, yes, the wages he offered were even less than I received from the del Amos—and, believe me, they were nothing to write home about. I was sorry for him, and anyway I only intended to stay until something could be arranged for his future care. You know how not with-it he is when it comes to noticing what goes on around him—remembering to eat—that sort of stuff.'

'Indeed.'

Izzy let out a huff of relief. He was beginning to believe her. She hated it when people thought badly of her—particularly him. Why him particularly? she wondered dazedly—and then the beginnings of exultation took a smart nose-dive.

'Yet you are here. Still with him. Even though you know his future wellbeing is secure, and when you have already said you intended to leave as soon as that situation arose. I wonder why that is?'

She could recognise the note of sarcasm

when she heard it. Izzy felt her skin crawl with the heat of discomfiture. Believing that honesty was the only policy, she mumbled, 'Well, I guess it might look odd. Only you *did* invite me. I told your uncle that as I was no longer needed I wouldn't tag along. But he refused to come if I didn't.' She raised her head, her eyes very wide, willing him to understand. 'You see, as I felt responsible for him, I guess *he* feels responsible for *me*.'

His gaze was calmly assessing. 'I see.'

Izzy swallowed jerkily. Did that mean he believed her? Had decided not to make her regret the day she was born?

Her bones turned to water when he gave her the benefit of his high-voltage smile and told her, 'I suggest you make yourself at home— rest until we meet at dinner. I will have a pot of English tea sent up to you.'

He walked out, his smile vanishing as he closed the door behind him.

She was devious and clever. She'd got her ingenuous patter down to a fine art. She could put on that look of earnest innocence and talk her way out of a double-locked and barred dungeon!

Only he wasn't gullible. His firm jaw set, he strode down to check on how his uncle was settling in, reflecting that her look of wide-eyed innocence didn't gel with the sexy body that oozed temptation.

His mouth tightened. Time to put his plan into action. Show her the sort of luxury she could only have dreamed of. Dangle the prospect of great wealth in front of her pretty nose. No need to actually bed her—just let her believe he wanted to, give her the impression that he was too much of a gentleman to take advantage of his uncle's companion. He would wait for her to get desperate enough to secure a massive fortune and openly encourage him, then make sure Miguel saw and understood what was happening—saw her in her true colours. Saw her as the greedy little sex-pot she was and hardened his highly moralistic heart against her.

Then Izzy Makepeace would be history!

Cayo laid down his dessert fork and leaned back in his chair, his smile just slightly apologetic. 'I asked for a simple meal. It's been a long day for you, Tio. Which is why I decided we wouldn't dress for dinner.'

Izzy, her mouth full of delicious ice cream layer cake, widened her eyes. If this had been a simple meal, then what would a lavish spread have been like?

Too hungry to be nervous—her stomach had been rumbling alarmingly when one of the maids had appeared at nine o'clock to escort her down to dinner—she had tucked in to a salad of roast peppers, then turbot fillets poached in wine, followed by slices of guinea fowl on a bed of tomatoes and onions, and ended with a pudding that had practically made her swoon!

And as for dressing down instead of up, as

would seem usual—well, she was already wearing her best: a plain blue cotton shift. Now she did feel nervous—even more so when Cayo remarked, apparently idly, as he toyed with the stem of his wine glass, 'As you might remember, Tio, at the end of this month I host the annual ball for my tenant farmers and estate workers, my business associates and their wives.'

'Indeed.' Miguel pushed his do-it-yourself repaired spectacles back up his nose. 'Am I expected to—as Izzy would doubtless say— strut my stuff?' He beamed at her and she gave back a hesitant smile, dreading the thought that she would be expected to put in an appearance at what would be a glittering event, and wondering if his High and Mighty Cayoness was busily chalking up another black mark against her for teaching his scholarly relative low-grade slang.

But, far from giving her that look of cold displeasure, he was actually smiling at her—just as he'd done before he'd left her room earlier. Maybe, she thought with a swoop of optimism, he had really thought about what she'd said and did believe her side of the story!

Her optimism increased by leaps and bounds when Cayo informed Miguel gently, 'It would be nice if you showed your face in the afternoon, when the locals are being entertained—you are often in their thoughts, and seeing you in your home setting at long last would give them pleasure. But if the evening events are too much for you to endure you may retire with my blessing.' His smile widened as his stunning eyes sought hers and held. 'No, I was thinking more about Izzy when I mentioned the coming celebrations. With the ball coming up in a fortnight she'll want to choose something glamorous to wear, and I need to be in Madrid tomorrow. I suggest she comes with me to find something suitable—that's if you can spare your companion for a couple of days?'

'Of course—an excellent suggestion! I shall be unpacking my papers and shall neither need nor want any help.'

So he *was* expecting Cinderella to go to the ball! Her heart headed for the soles of her feet, and with difficulty Izzy broke eye contact, biting down on her full lower lip. She could drown in those eyes, and was ashamed of the way he could make something pulse wickedly in the most secret part of her anatomy—especially when he was being nice to her, she thought in consternation as she felt her generous breasts tingle and push against the cotton barrier of her dress.

Aware that she was expected to say something, she wriggled uncomfortably in her chair and mumbled in agitation, 'Nice thought. But I'll pass. Thanks all the same.'

Refusing to be trapped by those dark Spanish eyes again, she gave her attention to Miguel as he asked, with his usual gentle humour, 'And why is that, *cara*? Do you carry a choice of sumptuous ballgowns in your rucksack?'

Mortified, Izzy's face blazed with embarrassed colour. 'You know I don't! I can't afford glamorous gear. But as I'll give the fancy ball a miss, there's no problem.'

Cayo's eyes swept her pink and mutinous face. Still playing games. Waiting for Miguel. He hadn't missed that telltale endearment; it had made his hackles rise. Well, he would give her what she was obviously waiting for. And then some.

He drained the last of his wine and set the glass back on the table, drawling, 'I don't live in the Dark Ages, expecting a relative's companion to be kept firmly out of sight on such an occasion! And as for your lack of funds—' A lean, tanned hand swept dismissively. 'Forget it. All that is necessary will be provided.' He sent her a look of sparkling challenge. 'It will be my pleasure.'

Izzy's tummy looped the loop, her face flushing. By the sound of it he had thought it over and decided to believe her side of the story! The hot surge of relief left her feeling weak. Although, she admitted, she shouldn't really care what he thought of her. They were nothing to each other. But at least it meant that he'd forgotten his hateful threat to make her regret the day she'd been born. He wouldn't be offering to take her to Madrid with him and buy her something suitable to wear if that was still on his agenda, would he?

Even so... 'I don't accept charity, *señor*.' Pride brought her chin up, leading to a collision course with those brilliant dark eyes. She compressed her soft, wide mouth as a throb of sexual awareness pulsed deep within her. She hated the physical effect he was having on her, but knew she could do nothing about it.

Her silly crush on Marcus had never left her feeling so helpless and out of control. Marcus had made her feel soft and gooey—motherly, even—worrying over whether he was feeding himself properly and wrapping up warmly when the north wind blew. She only had to look into Cayo's magnificent eyes to turn into a molten wreck!

'Charity doesn't come into it,' Miguel injected swiftly. 'You have been kind beyond words to a foolish old man. I am in your debt. And as I am still your employer I insist that you accompany my nephew.' He laid a gentle hand over hers in an affectionate gesture not unnoticed by Cayo's darkly glittering eyes. 'When you stepped in as my housekeeper I did you a grave disservice, as Cayo rightly pointed out. I was thoughtless and selfish. You will go to Madrid and allow Cayo to make amends on my behalf—to please me.'

Touched by that entreaty, Izzy felt her spine sag. She had grown very fond of the elderly man, and he was obviously beating himself up over his earlier absent-mindedness. The way she'd had to struggle to keep his household going on a pittance would have made a cat laugh. It had been a situation born not out of necessity or meanness, but out of his lack of interest in or knowledge of the world as it was today.

'Okay,' she agreed grudgingly. 'If it pleases

you.' She flushed with discomfiture as Miguel gave her hand a final squeeze and laid aside his linen napkin.

'Excellent! That's settled, then!'

But Izzy felt far from settled. Nerves were tingling all over her body. The prospect of spending time in Cayo's sole company made her feel dreadfully uneasy. And not because he harboured an ill will towards her, as had been the case until they'd had that talk earlier, but because for the first time in her life she was consumed by a deplorable lust for a man who was as far out of her league as the moon!

CHAPTER SIX

Lust could be conquered. Couldn't it?

Of course it could, Izzy reassured herself wildly as Cayo entered the sumptuous suite she'd been given through an interconnecting door that led, presumably, to his rooms. It was an intimacy she wasn't in the least ready for.

No need to get all hot and bothered, she assured herself shakily, trying her best not to look as agitated as she felt. He was now wearing a pale grey silk-sheened suit that screamed top designer and enhanced his wide shoulders, narrow waist, snaky hips and long, powerful legs with classy and understated elegance.

He took her breath away.

Tearing her eyes from him with difficulty,

she stared down at her toes. When he'd piloted the helicopter from Las Palomas to a private airstrip on the outskirts of Madrid he'd been wearing cargo pants and a torso-hugging sweatshirt, and she'd thought that she'd never seen a man who exuded such raw sexuality. She had spent most of the flight listening to his occasional comments through the headphones and telling herself to start thinking like a sensible adult. Admiring such a fine specimen of manhood was perfectly natural. But wanting—literally aching—to get up close and personal was right out of order.

Now, dressed as he was, the raw sexuality was still there in spades, but there was something extra. Power. Mastery. And that was scary—especially as her heart was racing, her pulses fluttering alarmingly, shameful hunger coiling deep in her pelvis.

She wished he'd say something to break the tension she could feel all around her, but when he did she wished he hadn't.

'If you're rested and ready, we'll go. I have a car waiting.'

Rested? Some hope!

She'd been pacing her room as if her legs had discovered the secret of perpetual motion ever since she'd arrived at this eye-poppingly luxurious hotel, which he'd casually informed her he owned—among loads of others. Part of his property portfolio, apparently. She'd been wondering what she was doing here, and beating herself up for so weakly agreeing to come in the first place. The leopard, it seemed, had changed his spots, and was being really, really nice to her. And she didn't think she could handle that because she could only just about keep her lustful yearnings under control when he was being vile.

And now he was suggesting—still in that warmly considerate tone—that if she was ready they were to go somewhere together.

She parted her lips to ask where, but all that emerged was an embarrassing croak. She cleared her throat, took a deep breath, avoided his stunning eyes and managed, 'I'll pass. You go. Wherever.'

Nice try, Cayo admitted grudgingly. Conversation had been limited on the helicopter flight, but she'd hung on his every word when he'd pointed out places and buildings of interest as the chauffeur-driven limo had whisked them through the suburbs and into the centre of the city. She had only withdrawn into her secret thoughts when he'd made sure she knew he owned the hotel they were to stay at. One of many throughout the world, and all of the same exquisite quality, he'd told her, as if he were used to vulgar boasting when nothing could be further from the truth.

In any other domestic servant he would have put her current subdued mood down to being out of her depth. But with Izzy Makepeace he knew better. She would be mentally totting up the value of this prime property, multiplying it by many, adding it to his export empire and licking her lips and planning tactics!

His chiselled mouth twisted wryly. But his drawl was smooth and soft as silk as he advanced, 'I don't think Madame Fornier would appreciate if it I attempted to try on the clothes she's laid aside in your stead.'

In dire danger of totally losing it, Izzy struggled to contain a sudden and alarmingly hysterical explosion of giggles at the picture that immediately presented itself—this ultra-masculine Spanish aristo trying to shoehorn himself into something several sizes too small, silky and slinky. Her eyes were sparkling with dancing laughter lights as she plucked her bulgy padded cotton handbag from the bed and slung it over her shoulder, stuffed her feet back into the spiky high heels she'd worn as a much-needed confidence booster, and announced, 'Fine. Let's go.'

Grab the first halfway suitable dress to wear to a ball she didn't want to attend and her ordeal would be over. They could head back to the castle and Miguel's easy, safe company. There was only so much of the magnificent Cayo Garcia's undiluted, sexy presence she could take without turning into a gibbering wreck of raging hormones.

Standing aside as she preceded him through the door, Cayo's eyes narrowed cynically as she swayed ahead of him at speed, on those ridiculously teetering heels. He deplored the way the enticing movement of her shapely backside awoke his most basic primal instincts, harshly reminding himself that the mention of a new wardrobe had got her moving as if she'd been shot from a cannon. Her big blue eyes had lit up like a Christmas tree at the thought of getting her hands on a whole bunch of freebies.

She couldn't hide her greed, he thought with dis-taste—then promptly reminded himself that her greed was what he was working on. Cocoon her in luxury, shower her with gifts, demonstrate what it was like to live in the lap of luxury, totally spoiled and pampered, and she would switch her avaricious attention from his clueless uncle to him. Mission accomplished.

And then Miss Izzy Makepeace would receive one large and unpleasant surprise.'

His wide, sensual mouth quirked with satisfaction as he caught up with her and laid a seemingly friendly arm across her narrow shoulders, guiding her towards the waiting car. 'It's not far. My driver will wait to take us on to the restaurant—we have a table booked for nine o'clock.' He eased her into the rear seat. 'He will then take your purchases back to the hotel.'

Leaning forward, he spoke rapidly in his own language to the driver, and as he settled himself beside her Izzy slid into the far corner. 'I could eat back at the hotel—have something in my room,' she objected.

She was already really, really nervous around him—terrified of the effect he had on her. Sharing dinner with him in some upmarket restaurant would be too much. Besides, dressed as she was, in a crumpled cotton skirt and one of her ordinary old T-shirts, she'd look horribly out of place. An excuse he'd understand, surely?

'I'd rather—honestly. And in any case I'm not dressed to go any place fancy,' she stressed as the car drew out into the early-evening traffic.

She stole a look at him from beneath long, fringing lashes and felt her heart stop, then flutter on. Angled from the corner, his eyes met hers. He was smiling. He was gorgeous! She felt dizzy.

'Nonsense.' His voice was like a slow, sexily warm caress. 'It is your first time in Madrid, yes? I insist you enjoy our city, and you won't do that by hiding in a hotel room.'

She had turned away from him now, her head downbent on the slender stalk of her neck, her glorious hair hiding her profile. But he wasn't falling for the shrinking violet act—just as he hadn't fallen for her story placing Augustin del Amo as the villain of the piece. It hadn't rung true.

He had no liking for the man, but he didn't

need a degree in psychology to understand that as a highly respected banker—regardless of his alleged discreet extra-marital tendencies—he would have far too much sense to foul his own nest. And Izzy Makepeace had been working for him, living under his roof.

Del Amo might have described her—accurately—as a 'lush little package', but with his business and social standing, and his wife's gimlet eyes on him, that would have been as far as it went. Del Amo might be many things he disliked, but he wasn't a fool.

Cayo snapped out of his thoughts as the car came to a stop. Relieving his driver of the necessity, he strode round to hand the tricky little madam out, reflecting that she wouldn't be able to hide her true colours when her greedy eyes fell on the delights Madame Fornier would have ready for approval.

His hand curved around her waist, urging her towards an arched doorway set in an elegant neo-classical building that looked nothing like any dress shop she had ever seen. Yet discreet gilded letters over the lintel announced 'Fornier' so she guessed, sinkingly, that it was some really fancy place where only the titled or extremely wealthy were admitted.

Izzy's skin prickled. She wished he wouldn't touch her. It made her feel quite dizzy! But at least, she comforted herself, he now believed her side of the del Amo story. He would still be being vile to her if he didn't—not nice, friendly and courteous, treating her to this trip to Madrid, a night in his fancy hotel and a new dress. The fact that he now didn't think the worst of her made her feel a little warmer inside. She was used to people finding fault— from her family to her past employers—so when someone was being nice to her she felt ridiculously like a tail-wagging, fawning dog!

And thinking of dogs—

Izzy dug her heels into the paving slabs. Not much more than a puppy. A miserable bundle of matted gingery hair and sticking-out ribs, cringing in the shadows of the archway, shivering in spite of the sultry evening heat.

'Oh, you poor little thing!' Izzy met the mournful brown eyes, registered the heart-rending whimper in response to her voice and was totally lost. Leaning forward, she scooped the pathetic little animal up. It wriggled ecstatically against her and nuzzled into the angle of her neck, its long, practically hairless tail furiously wagging.

Turning to Cayo, ignoring his frown, she stated, 'I can feel all his bones—he's starving!'

'And likely to be crawling with fleas. Put it down. Madame Fornier would not appreciate—'

'No.' Izzy stood her ground, her chin lifting stubbornly. No way was he going to make her abandon the needy puppy. 'I'm taking him back with me. He needs a bath and food. I can't just leave him here—pretend I haven't seen him. Even if you can!'

And then, because the Spaniard's frown had

deepened she added, less confrontationally, 'Look, don't think I'm not grateful for your offer of a new dress. I am. But I'm not bothered. I can live without a fancy dress, but this little thing won't last long unless someone cares for it. Pop in and apologise to Madame Whatever. Then we can take this poor little scrap back to the hotel.'

She actually meant it.

Cayo's spiralling perplexity deepened his frown still further. Had she been like this—five foot nothing of fierce protectiveness—when she'd stumbled across his uncle and the old man had collapsed? In that case she'd accepted a job at wages that were less than rock bottom in order to care for an old man she'd believed to be neglected and near destitute, caring for him when she'd thought that no one else did.

In this case she wasn't 'bothered' about acquiring a whole new wardrobe of designer gear. The immediate care of a scruffy mutt was of more importance.

Nothing seemed as clear-cut as it formerly had. Had he been wrong about her? Had his famous sound judgement let him down badly?

Moving forward, he set one final test. 'Does it have a collar or name tag?' Receiving a decisive and negative shake of her tousled blond head, he opined, 'Then I'm afraid it's been abandoned. I'll have my driver take it to a vet while we keep our appointment.'

As if the puppy had understood every word, it gave a piteous whimper and began licking Izzy's face. Her hands tightened protectively around the scrawny body. She could feel its little heart beating frantically. 'No!' She could just imagine a huge white-coated man with a lethal injection bending over the poor little thing. 'I can look after it!'

'Bueno!' Cayo's mouth firmed decisively. 'Wait in the car—and take that flea-ridden disaster with you.'

The last thing he needed in his life was a mangy puppy that would grow up into a mangy adult mongrel, but he knew when he was beaten and was practical enough to give way with good grace. Besides, for the first time in his adult life he felt as if he was on shaky ground, unsure of himself. He deplored the feeling.

Reaching into an inner pocket for his cell-phone, he made three short, tersely specific calls with the utter confidence of a man who was used to getting what he wanted, to having others jump when he told them to. Then he strode towards the waiting car, his eyes glinting narrowly as he sought an answer to the question of whether he'd been catastrophically wrong about Izzy Makepeace.

He was never wrong!

And yet…

Izzy's head was spinning and she couldn't stop grinning. She and the puppy had been treated like royalty ever since they'd arrived back at the hotel.

The manager had been waiting for them. Obsequious and deferential, he had accompa-

nied them up to her suite, barking out rapidfire
orders to two of his staff, who had filled a
plastic bath with warm water. To demonstrate
how important he was, the manager had
minutely inspected the bottle of baby shampoo
before handing it to her.

Aware of all eyes on her, of Cayo sardonically
distant in the background, Izzy had knelt and
lowered the puppy into the water. Benji, as
she'd already decided to name him, had taken
immediate exception to the unfamiliar experience and scrabbled frantically to escape the
unwanted dunking, soaking her and the
bathroom floor, and venting cross baby yelps
as she'd lathered and rinsed him, only subsiding when she had finally lifted him out and
wrapped him in the big fluffy towel immediately handed to her.

Leaving his staff to empty and remove the
bath, the manager had ushered her through to
the opulent sitting room, where a low table had
already been laid with a bone china plate of

thinly sliced chicken breast meat and a silver bowl of water.

Now, oblivious to the cleaners, who had arrived to put the bathroom back to its former pristine state, Izzy watched the puppy wolf down the chicken with enormous satisfaction, too pleased with the frankly amazing and gratifying outcome of what she had believed would be a huge problem to worry as a vet and his assistant arrived, bowed down with packages.

As Spanish seemed the order of the day, Izzy left the vet and his helper to their examination, contenting herself with exploring the packages, bulky and small. Cayo had arranged for the delivery of everything to make a small puppy happy and comfortable. There was a comfy padded dog bed, a soft blanket, a pack of puppy kibbles, feeding bowls and a minute collar and lead of the softest leather imaginable.

When the vet had finally made his departure Cayo lobbed a look—part exasperated, part amused—at Izzy, as she knelt over the dog bed, where the animal had finally settled.

Smiling, Izzy rose from her knees, turned and faced him, her hands on her curvy hips. 'You don't fool me, Cayo Garcia! You're nothing like as hard-hearted as you try to appear!'

Her huge eyes were glowing. They looked like priceless sapphires. The front of her T-shirt was soaked, moulding the thin fabric to every lethally voluptuous curve of her breasts.

His breath felt hot in his lungs. Whether or not she had mercenary intentions, whether she was a scheming, greedy gold-digger or a soft-hearted innocent in need of protection from her own headstrong, thoughtless altruism he had yet to discover. Only one thing was clear: she was a walking man-trap!

She was moving towards him, her luscious hips a swaying temptation, her smile wide and dazzling enough to make a man believe the sun had come out at darkest midnight. A small hand stretched out to him.

'He's really cute when he's asleep. Come and look. His name's Benji—'

'I'll pass.'

His voice sounded rusty. Something gave a violent wrench deep inside him. His face felt hot. Time to get out of here. Right now! He tore his eyes away from the temperature-raising outline of her nipples, the way the wet fabric clung.

'I suggest you get changed. I'll have dinner brought to you.' And he exited through the door that connected to his suite before he could give in to the shaft of driving sexual need that was invading his entire system.

CHAPTER SEVEN

IT FELT exactly like a blow between the eyes. Izzy blinked back the sudden sting of tears. For a few minutes she'd been feeling relaxed, even hopeful that her volatile relationship with Cayo could be somehow redefined, that there was at least an outside chance of an easy friendship between them—and who knew where that might lead? A girl could dream, couldn't she?

She'd almost—just fleetingly, of course, in a moment of insanity—believed herself to be falling in love with him!

How feeble could a girl get?

Disconsolately she plodded to the bathroom, stripped off her sodden clothes and had a quick shower. She took ages towelling herself dry, brooding over her lack of judgement.

The things he'd done to make sure the stray puppy received all necessary care had made her think that he'd transmogrified from the kind of guy who would walk past a starving small animal without batting an eyelash into someone who cared enough to summon vets, hotel managers and plates of chicken. A man with a kind heart.

How silly!

He'd only done it because he'd seen she'd been adamant about rescuing the puppy, and he hadn't wanted his precious hotel infected with fleas or to have to put up with her loudly wailing recriminations if the 'flea-ridden disaster', as he'd unflatteringly named poor Benji, had died!

And there she'd been, making a first unselfconscious friendly gesture towards him, wanting to share her pleasure with him, making a fool of herself, almost falling in love with him! And what had he done?

Flattened her!

Just as Marcus had done. The only difference being that Marcus had been Mr. Charming to her face, while ridiculing her behind her back and taking really hurtful advantage of her admittedly silly crush, and Cayo had been upfront, letting her know to her face that he wasn't interested in sharing a warm, happy moment with her.

Just what his reaction would be if she inadvertently allowed him to see that she fancied him rotten didn't bear thinking about!

Knowing her, and her inability to hide what she was feeling, that just might happen. She was going to have to be extra careful around him, she stressed firmly as she got into the complimentary bathrobe. She left the *en suite* bathroom to find that a tray of utterly delicious-looking food plus a bottle of wine had been left on one of the tables—a table that fronted one of the delicate antique sofas.

She poked glumly at the food, but she wasn't

hungry. So she poured herself some wine and, sipping, took it with her as she went to check on the puppy. He was still asleep. She almost wished he wasn't. She could do with some company.

She almost jumped out of her skin when a knock on the suite's door heralded the arrival of two porters with arms full of boxes which, smiling serenely, they deposited in a mountainous heap.

'For you, *señorita*,' the taller of the two explained, his accent thick. 'With the compliments of Señor Garcia.' They were both grinning at her now. Knowingly? Izzy's face flamed. Did they think she was the hotel owner's bit on the side?

Too mortified to be able to speak, even to say thank you, she watched them leave, swallowed the remainder of her wine in two thirsty gulps, and approached the boxes as if each and every one contained a time bomb.

They were matt black, with 'Fornier' inscribed in elegant gilt lettering. She felt so guilty she needed another gulp of wine. She smothered a giggle. The situation she'd gone and got herself into was turning her—she who rarely drank except the occasional small glass—into an alcoholic!

Poor *madame*! Because they'd failed to keep their appointment, Cayo had made the poor woman pack up the selection of dresses she'd been meant to choose from and had them sent over to the hotel. Didn't he care what trouble he put people to on his behalf?

Probably not.

Definitely not!

Well, the least she could do was make her choice now. Surely one out of what looked like a massive selection would fit? Not having laid eyes on her, *madame* would probably have covered all options, from lofty stick-insect to short, fat dumpling. Into which latter category she was afraid she would slot.

Unprepared for the reality, Izzy felt her eyes widen to saucers and her soft mouth drop open

as each lid she lifted revealed something different. From formal wear through to smart-casual,
exquisite underwear and dainty, kitten-heeled
shoes. Everything in her size. How had
madame known that? Had Cayo told her? Made
a wild and, as it happened, accurate guess?

Costly fabrics, sumptuous colours. Perfectly
cut, beautifully styled. The sort of garments
that would probably cost a king's ransom!

Her face set, her generous mouth mutinous,
she replaced the lids on all the boxes. She could
not, *would* not accept them.

Under mental protest she would accept one
dress to wear for the dratted ball. She wasn't at
all comfortable about that, but had reluctantly
gone along with it because Miguel, bless him,
wanted her to, and she could understand that
he'd been feeling bad about hiring her at slave-
labour wages.

Despite the air-conditioning she felt decidedly hot and bothered, and knew she'd never be
able to get a wink of sleep if she didn't tell

Cayo right now that this was all way over the top. No way was she going to allow anyone to spend such a large amount of money on her.

'You deserve only what you can pay for yourself. Anything else is freeloading. Look at James. He works hard. He's well on the way to being able to have exactly what he wants. The way you're going you'll be lucky to afford to keep yourself in those ridiculous shoes you insisted on wearing.'

It had been constantly drummed into her since she'd been a schoolkid, in an attempt by her parents to get her to achieve the unachievable—in her case high grades at school. Grades that would lead to that glittering goal: a high-paying, ultra-respectable career.

Cayo closed his cellphone, terminating the conversation with his chief accountant, citing the lateness of the hour as his reason for silencing the dry-as-dust voice. In reality he was completely unable to concentrate on the information he had asked for, disturbing the man in whatever he did to relax in the late evening.

Never before had he suffered from an inability to keep his mind on track. It was a first, and he knew who was to blame.

Izzy Makepeace!

His lean, strong features hardened. Had he made a serious error of judgement? To one who prided himself on rock-solid character assessment it was a possibility that sat uneasily on his broad shoulders. Recalling his initial treatment of her, the things he'd said, he flinched.

If he'd been wrong, then his behaviour had been reprehensible.

But had he?

True, earlier this evening she'd passed up acquiring a whole new wardrobe and dining at one of Spain's finest restaurants in favour of rescuing a stray puppy of the un-cute variety. If it had been an act to convince him that his opinion of her as a scheming, money-grubbing slut was way off the radar, then she was obviously a tragic loss to the theatre.

Striving for pragmatism, telling himself that only time would tell, that even now she would be trying on and drooling over the goodies he'd had the Frenchwoman send over, he crossed to the drinks cabinet and poured himself a sparing amount of Scotch.

Only to swing sharply round on the balls of his feet as the connecting door was flung open without ceremony and the object of his uncharacteristically muddled thoughts bounced in.

His grip tightened on his glass. Even with her bright mane of hair tumbling around her flushed face, her startlingly blue eyes narrowed and flashing like an angry cat's, and her luscious body bundled in a silk bathrobe, she was spectacularly sexy. His pulses quickened. He ignored them, deploring his body's sexual reaction to her.

Deplorable if he'd been right about her in the first instance, and just as deplorable if she turned out to be a wronged innocent.

He didn't bed innocents.

But he wanted to bed *her*?

Before that question could lead to an answer he wouldn't like, he lifted his proud dark head and ground out, 'What is it? Did you forget to knock?'

Sarcastic brute! There he stood, in all his male magnificence. Long legs planted firmly apart, his suit jacket shed, shirtsleeves rolled up to display the golden skin of his strong forearms, slightly roughened by fine dark hairs, with a lock of silky black hair falling forward to brush his arched, expressive brows.

Haughtily disdainful eyes.

She would never understand him in a million years! Nice as pie one moment; utterly vile the next. She had to be the world's biggest fool to fancy him. So she wouldn't, she told herself tipsily. She would say what she had come to say and then sweep out with dignity.

Looking at a point beyond his left ear, because she always went peculiar when she looked directly at him, she dragged in a deep breath and blurted, at volume, 'Send that stuff back! I'll pick out something to wear for that dance—sale or return, because I may not be around that long—but the rest's going back! I may not have two pennies to rub together, but I'm not on any registered charity list that I know about! And I'm not a freeloader, either!'

Satisfied that he'd got the message, she twisted round, took a giant stride in her haste to reach the connecting door, caught her bare foot in the hem of the swamping robe and fell on her face.

'Are you hurt?'

Tears of frustration, anger and downright mortification pooled in her eyes as strong hands fastened on either side of her waist and Cayo lifted her back onto her feet. She'd meant to be so dignified and decisive, and all she'd done was fall flat on her face in a heap!

Breath gathered in her lungs and stuck there, burning. Any minute now she was going to put the tin lid on it and burst into loud and messy tears—that was her chagrined thought as he turned her round to face him, repeating, 'Have you hurt yourself?'

His strong hands still steadied her, scorching through the silky fabric. He was so close—too close. She was stingingly aware of his lithe and powerful male body. An awareness that flooded her with tension.

Her heart began to pound heavily and she couldn't breathe. Against all common sense she lifted her eyes to his and felt exactly as if she were drowning in the soft dark depths.

Panicking, her knees threatening to give way under her, she reached out to clasp the strength of his forearms for support—and almost cried out in shock as the touch of warm skin sent a jolt of electrified sensation right through her body. 'I'm fine!' she gasped, dropping her hands and making a futile attempt to move away from him.

His hands tightening, Cayo held her still, his eyes surveying the downbent head with its mass of silky silver, and felt his heart jerk beneath his breastbone.

Her explosive entry into his room, the way she'd shouted at him—something no one had had the temerity to do for as long as he could remember—had forced a crooked smile of unwilling admiration to his sensual lips.

When she felt strongly about something— Tio Miguel, the scruffy mutt, a designer wardrobe most women would give their eyeteeth to be gifted—she stood up to him, waded in, fists metaphorically flying. It was refreshing after the immediate and simpering compliance of the sophisticated women who inhabited his social circle and bored him to distraction.

Gently, he used a long, tanned forefinger to lift her chin, forcing her to meet his eyes. Her full lower lip trembled ominously and the deep blue of her eyes shimmered with unshed tears. Hurt eyes, as clear and innocent as a child's.

Physically she was unharmed. But she was hurting. Self-contempt tightened his gut. He had wronged her, believed lies, dismissed her version of events out of hand, harbouring the unjust opinion that she had set out to weasel herself into his uncle's affections in order to get her hands on his fortune.

In all honour he had to make amends.

'We will sit and talk calmly—clear the air between us,' he announced, dropping his hand and taking one of hers in his. He led her through to the suite she was using, noting the untouched food and the opened bottle of wine. The scruffy puppy snuffling in the padded dog bed was beginning to wake.

Swallowing a sigh, he excused himself momentarily and picked up the house phone, his orders terse and clipped. His brows clenched together when he turned and saw that Izzy had squeezed herself into the corner of one of the sofas, her legs tucked up beneath her, her arms wrapped around her body, as if she were trying to make herself invisible. Her lovely face was troubled.

She was always putting her foot in it, Izzy thought wretchedly. Blindly charging in, all guns blazing, acting without thought—sensible or otherwise—making a great big fool of herself!

Small hands twisting in her lap, she wished she could become invisible. The unaccustomed intake of alcohol and the emotion of the day had heightened her crusading tendencies, and in the aftermath she could see that her wildly inappropriate response to the arrival of a load of horrendously expensive clothes that she would never have been able to afford for herself in a million years had been totally crass.

She should have done nothing, said nothing until the morning. And then informed Cayo—calmly and with dignity—that the gift was unacceptable. Left it at that, without all these diva-like histrionics.

There followed the prompt arrival of two uniformed members of staff—one bearing a loaded coffee tray and a plate of what looked like small crusty filled rolls, the other waiting for orders from Cayo, delivered in rapidfire Spanish. He lifted Benji from his basket, attaching the collar and lead to his scrawny neck.

'What's he doing?' Snapped out of her miserable introspection, and forgetting her lecture to herself, Izzy scrambled to her feet as the puppy was borne away.

In receipt of that suspicious reaction Cayo lowered his brows in annoyance. 'I think you should begin to trust me. The animal will be perfectly safe,' he informed her, with an extreme dryness that brought a bright flush of colour to Izzy's face. 'It is to be walked in the gardens of the hotel, to avoid accidents, and then taken to the housekeeper's room, where it is to be fed before being brought back.'

'Oh!' Izzy flushed uncomfortably and flopped back on the sofa. 'Sorry.'

'You jump to conclusions that do not flatter,' he imparted wryly as he lowered his lithe frame beside her. 'Why is that?'

'Why do you think?' He actually had the gall

to look mystified, Izzy decided. It was enough to make a cat laugh! But then, in his opinion, he could do no wrong. 'You said I should leave him where he was, and then you threatened to have him sent to a vet—probably to be put down. You didn't exactly encourage me to bring Benji back here, did you?'

'But I didn't prevent you,' he pointed out, the corners of his mouth twitching.

His statement floored Izzy, as she had to admit that since she'd refused to abandon the puppy he had done everything to ensure its comfort and wellbeing—even though he was clearly not a fan of small animals with mangy-looking hair and stubby legs.

'Enough of that. We have other, more important things to discuss.' A lean, tanned and beautifully crafted hand sliced dismissively. 'The dog is yours.'

Izzy instinctively turned to thank him, to look directly at him, and her tummy flipped. He was so handsome he took her breath away. She wished quite desperately that he'd take himself off to his own suite, because she so wanted to move closer than the scant inch or two that separated them, to reach up and pull that handsome head down, to feel his beautiful mouth against hers… And if she wasn't very careful she'd find herself doing just that, making a monumental fool of herself…

Cayo shifted uneasily, unable to take his eyes from her lovely face. The beautiful blue eyes no longer looked innocent and childlike but sultry, the dark, gold-tipped lashes lowered. Her soft full lips parted, pink and inviting. The ache at his groin intensified. His pulses went into overdrive. He raised an unsteady hand to brush aside the tendril of silky silver hair that had tumbled over her wide forehead but, appalled by the thoughtless impulse, swiftly dropped it again.

Getting sharply to his feet, he incised, 'As the meal was not to your liking and is now cold you must help yourself to coffee and rolls. I'll see you in the morning. As I said, there are things to discuss.' And he left with as much haste as his condition would allow to seek a long cold shower.

She had her wish, Izzy acknowledged, stunned by his abrupt and curt departure. He was seeking his own suite and no doubt locking the door! So why did it feel as if she'd been drenched with a bucket of freezing water?

He'd probably legged it because she'd been looking at him as if he were a juicy steak and she was starving, she admitted with deep embarrassment. Around him, especially when he was being okay and not calling her names or threatening her with goodness knew what because he thought she was after his uncle's money, she couldn't help herself.

Feeling drained and ridiculous, she wandered over to pour herself a cup of coffee, and sat to await the puppy's return.

The only sensible thing to do was to take herself off, out of his orbit, and find work, hopefully with accommodation thrown in. Some place where a small puppy would be tolerated.

He'd said there were things they had to discuss. Well, her departure, as soon as possible, would be top of the list.

CHAPTER EIGHT

THE second of his two tiresome but apparently necessary business calls returned and completed, Cayo crossed to the bank of tall windows and flung them wide open. At this time of year Madrid sweltered beneath an unforgiving brassy sun, sending those Madrileños who could heading for cooler coastal or mountain climes.

But this early in the morning the temperature was bearable, and he filled his lungs with the last of the cool air he could expect to enjoy today, looking with wry affection out over the rooftops of the uncompromisingly modern city. Big and busy, it offered its fair share of culture in the form of museums, theatres and opera. And the rare treasures of the Royal Palace and its elegant parks, and sophisticated entertainment such as nightclubs and restaurants were second to none.

A consumer's paradise, and a rich feeding ground for the likes of gold-diggers—as he'd first named his uncle's housekeeper.

Unfairly blackening her character?

Maybe.

Almost certainly.

The thought did nothing to make him feel good about himself.

A few days—a week if he stretched it—of allowing Izzy Makepeace to wallow in the best the city had to offer, showing her that at his side the world was her oyster, or could be, was now unthinkable. At least not for the reasons that had led to his initial plan.

But as a way of making amends it was doable. Right. That was if he had anything to make amends for.

He couldn't remember a single time in all of his thirty-three years when he had fallen prey to indecision. He weighed up known facts and made up his mind. And that was that. No ifs and buts.

But in Izzy's case he damn well wasn't sure. He'd lain awake half the night reviewing the known and conflicting facts, and still, to his chagrin, he hadn't reached a rock-solid unarguable conclusion.

Was she, as the events of the last twenty-four hours would appear to suggest, innocent of all he had mentally and verbally accused her of being? Or was she just diabolically clever and a remarkably fine actress into the bargain?

Only time would tell.

Despising himself for what in others he would have named a deplorable weakness of character—an unprecedented and decidedly uncomfortable emotion, and one he wasn't prepared to live with for much longer—he flung open the connecting doors to her suite. They would continue the discussion he'd aborted the previous evening, and he would winkle out as many facts about her as he could.

He stood, straddle-legged, on the threshold of her suite. Of what looked like her *empty* suite, he noted scowlingly.

He called her name. It hung, unanswered, on the still air.

Last night she had approached him with a warm and gorgeous smile that could prove to be an unwary man's downfall, her hand outstretched in invitation. Inviting him to coo over her new pet! The naïve action of an innocent, or a calculated prelude to something far more earthy?

Madre de Dios! All he'd wanted to do, burned to do, was to sweep her into his arms and strip away the silky robe, revealing himself to be as excited as a kid tearing the wrappings from a wickedly tempting package on Christmas morning!

Recognising danger came instinctively to him. He'd made some brusque remark and left her. Likewise, earlier, when he'd escorted her back to her suite, he'd been drawn into the sudden sultry mystery of her eyes and felt himself to be drowning, wanting to explore the mystery, draw her to him, taste her, know her.

Thankfully he'd had the strength of mind to distance himself smartly from temptation, because on the one hand he didn't make love to greedy tramps and on the other he didn't seduce an innocent—especially an innocent he'd already wronged.

Either way, Izzy Makepeace was strictly out of bounds! And this morning they had things to discuss. She knew that. He'd made it plain. He vented an expletive beneath his breath. When he made arrangements he expected them to be adhered to—to the letter!

That had to be why this almost frantic sense of frustration was claiming him after a search of the entire suite revealed nothing. Apart from the empty dog bed, and the neatly stacked Fornier boxes that had the air of rejection about them, Izzy might never have been anywhere near these rooms.

He ran lean fingers through his midnight hair, his scowl deepening as he reached for the phone and dialed down to the manager—to learn that the Señorita had been seen walking the small dog in the grounds of the hotel. Early. About an hour ago, or maybe longer.

An hour!

The hotel grounds were beautifully tended, tranquil, but nowhere near extensive enough to hold her interest for an hour or possibly more. Had she grown bored and set off into the city with that ridiculous puppy? Totally forgetting that he would be expecting her to be in her suite, waiting for him to join her?

Just another aspect of her thoughtless behaviour.

His features set in grim lines. On the whole, Madrid was a relatively safe place, but there were areas of the city where it was definitely unsafe for a lone female to venture. And this lone, sexy female wouldn't have a clue as to where she was going. She barely spoke half a dozen words of the language, and those in an accent so excruciating as to be unintelligible.

His heart was pumping fit to burst out of his chest as he brushed past a startled waiter and bounded through the wide French windows onto the terrace a scant four minutes later.

Nothing. A couple of early risers drinking coffee at one of the terrace tables. The sweep of emerald-green lawn beyond, empty of any strolling, lush little lady with a ragged, stumpy-legged dog on a lead.

Unless…

His long, loose-limbed stride took him over the immaculate grass in double-quick time, past a stand of oleanders towards the walled perimeter, where a deep belt of parasol pines cast welcome shade and filtered out the noise of traffic.

If she wasn't down here he would have to scour the city streets, and when he found her he would take a great deal of pleasure in wringing her little neck for doling out such unacceptable measures of anxiety!

After the glare of the sunlight the shade was dark as Hades, and he allowed his eyes a few moments to adjust before he strode deeper, calling her name with growing irritation. He swallowed a full-throated, anger-filled roar as a small, sparsely-haired missile hurled itself at him, stubby legs working overtime, lead trailing, and fixed him with bright beady eyes, the tail wagging the body.

Gritting his teeth, Cayo bent to grab the lead. Where the mutt was, its owner wouldn't be far away. Doing what? Wasting his time!

'Find!' he commanded, without much hope. Without any, actually. In his estimation the animal's intelligence would be on a par with its looks. Zilch!

Hanging on to the lead for grim life as the little dog shot off like a greyhound out of a trap, Cayo wondered if once again he'd been mistaken. Did the animal have enough intelligence to be heading for his mistress, or was it careening off in any direction just for the heck of it? And then he saw her.

Sitting on the bone-dry earth, one leg tucked beneath her, rubbing the ankle of the other. Her washed-out denim skirt was rucked up to thigh level. She had lovely legs, firm rounded thighs—the sort of thighs a man could dream of moving between.

Anger at his entirely inappropriate line of thought made his voice sharp as he lashed out. 'What do you think you're doing? We had things to discuss this morning. Did you forget? Or were you born lacking in common courtesy? And what's wrong with your ankle?' he added after a beat of breath. Eyes narrowing, he moderated his tone—because he recognised that his harsh verbal onslaught stood in the stead of the more physical and metaphorical promised pleasure of wringing her dainty little neck!

He'd been worried about her—anxious on her behalf. The thought that she might have taken herself out of the hotel grounds and got herself lost in a city that could present danger to a solitary and unwary female had she wandered into one of the more unsavoury areas had made him taste fear for the first time in his life.

Over the top, he recognised with shaming hindsight. Totally. He didn't feel *that* protective of her!

Did he?

Madre de Dios, he was losing his marbles! Ever since she'd been around he'd been losing his fabled cool! And now she was just sitting there, cuddling the ugly pup who was frantically licking her face, ignoring *him*!

Planting his feet apart, he bit out in his best boardroom-silencing tones, 'I asked you a question. What is wrong with your ankle?'

Emerging from the excess of doggy devotion that had gone some way to compensate for His Lordship's yelling at her, Izzy tossed back her head, setting the wild silky exuberance of her long hair flying, and answered as coolly as her crossness at being unfairly bawled out would permit.

'Nothing much. I tripped, and twisted it a bit.

But it's much better now. Thank you for asking,' she added with an injection of sharp sarcasm, setting Benji back on the ground and hoping she could get to her feet without any real lack of dignity. She paused to lob at him, 'I thought it was more than early enough to get a walk in before you surfaced. I didn't twist my ankle on purpose, and I didn't ask you to inconvenience yourself and come to look for me. So don't snap and snarl at me! I can't think what we have to discuss anyway, although I hadn't forgotten. But might I suggest you make a proper appointment in future? You know—state a time and place, for example!'

She glared up into his lean, darkly handsome face and immediately wished she hadn't. He did things to her that should be prohibited by law. And he was trying not to smile. That made it worse—made hot tears of anger well into her eyes. She was telling him off, being serious, and he thought she was funny!

Desperate to hide her reaction—the pulse-racing physical desire that flooded her whenever she was around him, or even thought about him, come to that—she scrabbled awkwardly to her feet, biting her lip and clumsily hopping on one foot. Because her wretched ankle did still hurt. She hoped he didn't see the way her colour came and went. She couldn't control the way heat exploded deep in her pelvis and made her feel weak and fluttery all over. It was a source of shame to her and she'd just die if he guessed what he did to her.

'Here—' Strong hands reached out to steady her, spanning her small waist. Her head was lowered, the silvery blond curls all over the place. He had the finger-itching impulse to run his hands through the shimmering strands, to lift swathes of it to his face and breathe in the faint flowery perfume of it. Instead he asked with commendable, drawling cool, 'Can you put all your weight on that foot?'

Beast! Izzy's head shot up, angry tears once

more flooding her eyes. Did he have to state the obvious? That she was overweight! She'd never be a size zero, but did he have to rub her nose in it?

'It really hurts?' Cayo supplied softly. The sight of her tears was making his heart clench, and he surprised himself with a genuine wish that he could take whatever pain she was feeling away from her and bear it himself.

Suddenly his heart felt like marshmallow. Just because there were genuine tears sparkling in her beautiful eyes? Could a man of his age go senile?

'Don't cry.' Where had that husky note come from? A frown darkened his brow. Stamping hard on the pressing urge to drop his head, close her eyelids with his lips, kiss the tears away, then trail a route down to her lush pink mouth, feel her lips parting for him, inviting him, to touch her with his hands, all of her, he gritted his teeth. He ignored the insistent ache in his groin and lifted her into his arms, striding back through the trees, the little dog trotting in his wake.

Izzy gasped as her whole body melted into his strong arms, her breathing shallow and erratic. The huffy disclaimer that her angry tears had nothing to do with the discomfort in her ankle and everything to do with his obliquely pointing out that she was a stranger to any regime of dieting and strenuous work-outs had disappeared at the speed of light.

Held by him, this close to him, their combined body heat seemed to ignite into a violent sexual conflagration, turning her mind to mush and her body to a quivering, needy wreck. She expelled a shaky moan, wound her arms around his neck and snuggled her head into his hard-muscled shoulder, wallowing in illicit sensational excitement, almost exploding with it as they reached the sun-drenched lawns.

He said, with an intensity that scorched what little was left of her brain, 'I'll get someone to look at that ankle.' And then, coming out of nowhere, 'And then I'll kiss it better myself. Would you like that?'

* * *

Kiss it better? Would she like that?

Would she like to win the Lottery and as a bonus discover the secret of eternal youth?

She knew to her everlasting shame that she would like him—absolutely *love* him—to kiss every inch of her body. Her face flamed with acute mental discomfort. She who had never had any trouble holding on to her virginity, never given that state a thought, wanted him, this gorgeous man, to take it from her.

So what did that make her?

Incredibly stupid, she supplied with self-loathing. 'Kiss it better'? Get real, girl! He'd said the sort of thing people the world over said to humour any child suffering some minor hurt.

So he was treating her like a child now, was he? An overweight child! He had the knack of making her so angry she wanted to throw things—straight at his arrogant, too-handsome head, preferably! He was the only person in the whole world who could turn her normally good-natured placid self into a seething, emotional wreck! Reduce her to wanting to boil him in oil and make mad, passionate love to him at the same time!

As far as she was concerned he was incredibly dangerous. How long would it be before she made a monumental fool of herself? Letting him know that she was so in lust with him she didn't know what to do with herself?

He'd either laugh till his head dropped off or shoot her one look of grim distaste and make sure he never came within a hundred miles of her ever again!

True, he seemed to have changed his mind about her being a gold-digger without a moral worth mentioning. But that didn't mean he'd be over the moon if he realised an overweight, poorly dressed domestic servant wanted to get up close and personal with an elevated being such as he.

The only thing to do was take herself off, *pronto*. She would insist Cayo took her back to his lofty luxurious castle and then explain to Miguel that she didn't want to be a companion. If he decided to return to Cadiz at the end of the summer he'd have to find another housekeeper. It would, of course, mean failing at yet another job, she thought disconsolately as she stared at her bound ankle on the footstool.

At least there was no real damage there. Cayo had magicked a doctor out of thin air, seemingly. No surprise there, then. People jumped when he told them to, pausing only to tug at their forelocks and ask, *Please, sir, how high, sir?*

A slight sprain, that was all. The doctor had deftly bound the offending ankle, given instructions that she was to stay off it as much as possible for the remainder of the day, and then Cayo had slid the footstool beneath her foot and left with the elderly medic. Leaving her to stew in her self-declared mania. And fume.

Until: 'We both missed breakfast.'

Izzy's heart thumped wildly as Cayo entered

the room, complete with loaded tray, and the simmering, sexy smile that increased her inner turmoil by rocket-propelled miles produced a self-protective snipe. 'Do-it-yourself time, is it? No platoon of waiters and managers and fanfares—?'

'Shut up.'

His dark eyes were liquid. Warm. Dressed now in a fresh, startlingly white shirt, and hip-hugging dark trousers that made his legs look endless, he was a menace to the female sex, Izzy accused mentally as she watched his lithe movements. He placed the tray on a low table by her side and swung a delicate gilded chair to place it within touching distance. There was a trite phrase, wasn't there? 'Poetry in motion'? Trite or not, it just about cut it.

She expelled a long sigh. One minute she'd been a bundle of fuming disgruntlement because he'd left her alone, and the moment he showed his face she went all unnecessary!

Pouring dark, fragrant coffee, Cayo handed

her a cup. It rattled on the saucer as she took it. Poor scrap!

Leaving with the doctor, he'd done what he should have done days ago. Put through a call to Augustin del Amo. His tone had held threats that hadn't needed to be voiced—because no one who had a thought for his future peace of mind refused to co-operate when Cayo Angel Garcia demanded it. He had quickly obtained the truth that lay behind Izzy's summary dismissal from the household.

A truth he had been increasingly convinced of himself.

Now all he had to do was try to make amends.

He hooked a chair closer to the one she was using. Sat.

'I have something to tell you, Izzy. And something to ask you.'

CHAPTER NINE

GRITTILY determined not to let him get his word in first, to sidetrack her, Izzy gulped down her coffee without tasting it. One second in his company was enough to knock her common sense clear over the boundary and scatter her resolve to the four winds, so the sooner she made her intentions known the better.

'I'm leaving—can you get me back to Las Palomas, please?' She practically babbled in her haste to get her self-protective, set-in-concrete decision voiced.

She didn't look at him in case she turned to jelly, as she always did. She kept her eyes glued to the puppy, who was lying on his back, snoring, hoping the gods would be kind and help her find a job and a place to live where pets would be welcome.

'So soon?' Cayo disposed of his empty cup with care, one flaring ebony eyebrow lifting. 'But you've seen nothing of the city,' he pointed out mildly, wondering what had brought this on. 'Madrid has much to offer.'

His narrowed dark-as-midnight eyes searched what he could see of her averted features. He learned nothing beyond the obvious: something had rattled her cage. It was the first time he had encountered a female he couldn't immediately read like a tediously boring book.

Unless, of course, her ankle was still painful. That might explain her grouchy mood. Though he had been assured that the sprain was slight. Or maybe she thought—wrongly—that she was to be incarcerated in this room, with her foot stuck on a stool, for the duration of her visit to the capital.

Satisfied that he had found the answer with

his usual incisiveness, he imparted, with the smoothness of silk, 'You don't have to spend all your time cooped up in a hotel room. We'll hit the town later. You won't be up to sightseeing or dancing the night away—not for twenty-four hours, anyway—but a superb meal and a glass or two of fine champagne in one of the city's premier restaurants might put a smile back on your face. And it will give you the opportunity to try out something from your new Fornier wardrobe.' It was the least he could do after what he had learned from the sleazy apology for a man Augustin del Amo.

The smile in his voice curved his mouth as he waited for her response, fully expecting to enjoy the radiance of her gorgeous smile as she accepted that invitation. Of course he wasn't smug! The satisfaction he felt was down to confirming that he hadn't lost his touch. He'd always been able to second-guess what other people were thinking—a knack that had proved its worth in gold in his business dealings.

Had he been standing, he'd have been rocked back on his heels when she turned her head and gave him a look overflowing with frustration and loathing, and bawled, 'How shallow can you get?'

Telltale patches of hectic colour adorned her cheeks. She felt so wound up she was in danger of exploding. Did he think all she wanted to do was to flounce around in designer dresses and swill champagne? 'I wasn't talking about leaving this *room*! I meant your uncle's employ, and possibly even Spain! Like *now*, or sooner!' Her deep blue eyes were sparkling with tears of rage.

She'd screwed herself up to the point of accepting that she had to do the sensible, properly adult thing and remove herself from his dangerous presence—even though knowing she'd never see him again made her feel sick and empty inside—and his only and no doubt predictable response was to react as though she were the idiotic, empty-headed child he obviously thought she was, easily placated by the offer of a treat!

But he didn't know how she felt, she admitted, subsiding, always the first to see the other side of a story. He didn't know—couldn't know—that she only had to set eyes on him to be wanting to rip his clothes off. And her own!

'I see.' Cayo's eyes narrowed as he swiftly recovered from the shock of having been proved wrong. An event as rare as finding a lap-dancing nun! There had to be some kind of witchery about this lady, because she'd done the unthinkable and proved him wrong all along the line.

So she was definitely planning to walk away from her job as Miguel's housekeeper-cum-companion? So why was his brain already formulating objections when seeing the back of her was what he'd been so desperate to achieve since he'd learned she was working for his uncle?

And why had the bellowed information immediately put him in direct opposition, just as diametrically determined to keep her around?

But wanting to see the back of her had been

then. This was now, when he knew the truth, he rationalised. He had an international reputation for hard-nosed ruthlessness, but had always believed he was fair-minded. He didn't want her to leave without some recompense for the hard time he'd given her when he'd taken the words of the banker and his wife at face value.

He couldn't forget the way she'd set to and looked after Miguel, working hard for slave-labour wages just to see that an old man she thought was on the breadline was comfortable and cared for. That alone, in his book, demonstrated a rare generosity of spirit, and deserved reciprocal generosity on his part.

Relieved that he'd worked that out, and that his initial shattering reluctance to see her pack her bags and walk away had nothing to do with his regrettable difficulty in keeping his hands off her, he relaxed. Lust he could deal with. No problem. But his conscience wouldn't let him see her leave before he'd made adequate recompense.

Swinging himself to his feet, he removed the breakfast tray. Neither of them had touched the fruit or the linen-wrapped hot crusty rolls. No matter. Eating was low on his list of priorities at the moment. She'd been loudly vehement in her stated desire to leave his uncle's employ—'now or sooner'.

He would change her mind. Tio Miguel would expect it of him. He would be vastly upset if she were to leave with no job to go to and nowhere to live, just her clothes bundled into a rucksack and a scruffy mutt on the end of a lead. Or so he excused his own bone-deep reluctance to wave her off at a bus stop.

'There is surely no hurry?' The words slid out like warm honey as he returned to her side, leaning forward to scoop her effortlessly into his arms. Ignoring her spluttered protest, he strode through the open long windows, out of the air-conditioning and into the blaze of white heat on the wide balcony.

Izzy, her heart beating so fast she felt giddy,

pummelled his broad chest with ineffectual fists. Being swept up into his arms twice in one morning was seriously undermining her sanity, and making the secret feminine part of her throb, ache, turn moist and slick. She was so ashamed of herself that an anguished sob escaped her before she could swallow it.

'You are overwrought.' Cayo gentled her into a padded seat. 'There really is no need.' He adjusted the huge sun awning so that she was completely in shade, withdrew his mobile from a pocket at his narrow hips and issued rapidfire orders in his own language, smiling down at her.

His black eyes were liquid with kindness, and Izzy looked quickly away, concentrating on the view out over the gardens until her eyes stung. Because meeting his gaze, holding it, would let him read what was there: desire, lust, need—the whole package. She wouldn't let that happen.

So she was overwrought! Whose fault was that? The sex-on-legs man who was now telling

her, 'Cold drinks will be with us in moments.'
That was who!

He was also saying, 'We must talk. But first
I want to apologise. I accused you of trying to
wheedle your way into Miguel's affections
with the intention of getting your hands on his
wealth, of having no morals worth mentioning.
I was wrong.'

Izzy's soft pink mouth dropped open, her
huge eyes wide as she watched him move
forward and join her on the padded seat, one
arm disposed along the back. She wouldn't
have thought his inbred arrogance would
permit him *ever* to admit to being in the wrong.
She'd assumed that apologies would be a
stranger to his tongue—he hadn't apologised
when she'd given him her version of the events
that had led to her dismissal from her former
job, so why was he saying sorry now?

She angled her head to one side, gazing up at
that compellingly handsome face, and Cayo
caught his breath between his teeth.

Her enchantingly tousled hair was tumbling forward in a tangle of shimmering silver-blond curls. His fingers ached to make exploratory contact. And her parted lips, lush, moist, rose-pink, were an invitation he was hard pushed to resist. And those clear, unbelievably blue eyes—

He cleared his throat roughly, his tone husky and then flattening as he confessed, 'I spoke to Augustin del Amo this morning.' He thought it wise to admit the truth of what really happened. 'Again, I can only apologise, and ask you to allow me to make some reparation.'

His accent was more pronounced than she'd ever heard it, and a lock of silky black hair had fallen forward to brush his arched, expressive brows. He reached out and took her hands. Her ability to breathe vanished. The golden skin of his forearms was slightly roughened by fine dark hairs. So temptingly touchable…

A great choking lump took residence in Izzy's throat. A question burned her tongue.

The electrifying touch of his hands on hers sent it flying out of her head.

He repeated his request, 'May I make reparation?'

She could only gasp, 'Such as?'

His mobile mouth twitched. Izzy wanted to kiss it so much it made her insides fizz. Which was why she had come to the grown-up decision to leave as soon as humanly possible, she reminded herself. A decision that was founded on very shaky ground, she discovered, when his long tanned fingers tightened around hers and he supplied, 'A billion sterling in a diamond-encrusted gold crate, perhaps?'

Laughter lights in both dark velvet and sparkling blue eyes met and melded.

'You remembered that!'

'How could I forget? You are the only woman I know to let me feel the sharp edge of her tongue.'

'I bet!' She tugged her hands away from his. The fleeting moment of rapport had vanished.

It had felt so very good. But now it might never have happened. She wished it hadn't!

Long, gold-tipped lashes swept down to veil her eyes, because it really hurt to translate what he meant. Hordes of beautiful, sexy, exquisitely dressed, sophisticated and suitable women flattering him outrageously and hanging on his every word. Not a single one with any reason or desire to even think about bad-mouthing him!

Mental images of some nameless, long-legged lovely wrapped all around him, cooing sweet nothings and purring with pleasure, rose up to choke her, blinding her to the arrival of a waiter with the cold drinks Cayo had ordered.

With a brief nod of thanks he leaned towards her, his eyes soft, and assured her, 'That was a compliment, *amada.*'

Stop it! she shrieked inside her head. When he was nice to her, her emotions went haywire! Her hand shaking, she lifted a glass, her fingers curling around the ice-cold surface. She drank the most refreshing grapefruit juice she'd ever tasted as if she were stranded in a desert and dying of thirst.

Setting the empty glass back on the table with unnecessary vigour, Izzy wished she were impervious to Cayo's charismatic good-looks, but she knew she never would be—not in a million years.

She was thrown completely off-balance when he captured her hand and said, in that slow, sexy drawl, 'Time to talk. As friends.'

Her hand felt so small and delicate within his, her fingers curling in response. He had the unprecedented and urgent need to lift it to his mouth, plant kisses deep within her palm.

He didn't do soppy, romantic gestures!

And he wasn't going to start with Izzy. Izzy was out of bounds!

Which was a pity!

Scrub that thought!

His features as impassive as only he could make them, he gently untwined her fingers from his and carefully replaced her hand back on her lap. 'You up for it?'

'For what?' Her voice sounded funny, as if she were drunk, Izzy decided. Just because he'd briefly held her hand again. Time to get a grip.

'I want to discuss your decision to leave Miguel's employ.'

'Oh. Right.' Izzy perked up. At least she told herself she did. She'd made the perfectly sensible and correct decision to leave, and naturally Cayo would want to discuss the best way to go about getting her back to Las Palomas, as she'd requested, where she could pack the remainder of her gear and say her farewells to Miguel. 'Go ahead.'

'I understand your decision to leave,' Cayo assured her gently, determined to prevent her taking off like a scalded cat. He wanted her to leave Las Palomas only when he had decided his guilt over his shockingly bad judgement had been relieved. 'His work's the only companion Tio Miguel needs, always has been, and as it's my firm intention to get him to agree to make Las Palomas his permanent home he won't need a housekeeper. Staying in his employ would make you feel like a spare part.'

Izzy nodded her agreement, the sudden painful lump in her throat not allowing her to vocalise. He understood, and he would do everything in his considerable power to facilitate her removal from the lives of the super-elevated Garcias with all haste.

Deflation hit her. A decision made in a blinding moment of unadulterated common sense was one thing. But being faced with the imminence of a very uncertain future, with the responsibility of a small puppy to add to her anxieties, was quite another. Perhaps common sense wasn't all it was cracked up to be.

Sparkling dark eyes enhanced by incredibly thick black lashes rested on her slightly trembling pink mouth. 'I won't ask you to alter your decision, only to delay it.'

He caught his breath as she lifted her eyes to his. So wide, so vulnerable. The thought of her, jobless, homeless, wandering Spain in the hope of picking up work, was inconceivable. He wouldn't let it happen. He might be the tough nut described in the financial papers, but he wasn't a monster.

'Give it a couple of weeks or so—at least until after the Summer Ball. Leave straight away and Miguel's feelings would be hurt—especially if you ungraciously refuse to accept the new wardrobe he specifically wanted you to have. I know he feels badly about the way he so grossly underpaid you, and I know he wants you to have a holiday. And as for me—' he spread his finely made hands expressively '—I owe you. It's not beyond my capabilities to find you suitable work and accommodation within one or other of my companies.' Not a shadow of his ongoing loathing at the thought of seeing her walk off into the sunset with no visible form of support showed on his face as he invited, 'Tell me of your life before you came to Spain.' Miguel had told him what he knew, what she'd confided. He wanted to know more.

'Why?' Izzy swung her legs around and wriggled into a position where she was directly facing the man seated at her side. She caught her breath, mesmerised by the sheer brilliance of his eyes, horribly aware of the tightening tingle of awareness deep in her tummy. Was he, at last, actually interested in her as a human being? A woman?

It was a thought too sweet to be ousted by acknowledging its sheer stupidity—until he countered blandly, 'Think of it as a job interview. If I'm to place you within one of my companies I need to know I'm not trying to push a round peg into a square hole.'

Extreme humiliation claimed her. No wonder her family was irritated by her, called her stupid. Of *course* he wasn't interested in her as a flesh-and-blood woman. Why the heck should he be? She had none of the social graces, the dazzling beauty and sophistication that would raise a flicker of interest in a man such as he.

Squashing the desire to tell him to mind his

own business, that she'd find work without his help, she glumly acknowledged that she couldn't afford to be defiant just because her feelings had been hurt. Feelings she had had no right to have in the first place. Talk about cutting her nose off to spite her face! She needed work. He'd promised to place her.

'My CV's nothing to write home about,' she mumbled, her hands twisting in her lap with sheer embarrassment.

Her family had always drummed it into her that unless she applied herself academically she would get nowhere. Wrongly, she decided with hindsight. Because she had always known she could never begin to approach the scholarly brilliance of her older, doted-upon brother, she hadn't even tried. Now she was being obliged to spell it out.

'No qualifications. A string of going-nowhere jobs. And then Dad found me work in his office—he was a solicitor. Just making the tea, really, and running errands. Then he retired—'

'To New Zealand, to be with your doctor brother.'

'James is a brilliant surgeon,' Izzy corrected, knowing full well her brother would have insisted on that distinction. She pinkened because Miguel must have told him this stuff, which reminded her that Cayo would have been checking out his uncle's new and—in his initial opinion—dodgy housekeeper. Miguel would have relayed what he knew about her because she'd confided heaps about her background to explain what she'd been doing in Spain in the first place.

'And you took work in Spain, leaving your job and your home because you and the man you were in love with had a falling out.'

Cayo cut to the chase. It figured. She could be fiery-tempered, headstrong enough to act on impulse without calmly thinking out the consequences. But she was also warm-hearted, and hadn't a mean or ungenerous bone in her delectable body.

'Are you still in love with him?' It was a struggle to keep his tone uninterested when he was illogically incensed by the possibility— for some reason he was totally at a loss to understand.

He was left clenching his teeth against some unwise and possibly ridiculous frustrated outburst when, her chin up, she came back with, 'That is absolutely none of your business!'

Miguel obviously hadn't relayed the whole story of her soppy crush on Marcus, the way he had used her and laughed at her behind her back, and she certainly wasn't going to lay what amounted to her further stupidity and humiliation on the table for him to gloat over or pity her for.

'I take that as a yes.' The dismissive tone he could turn on at will was at odds with what he could only describe as his anger. Miguel had been short on details of the English love of his housekeeper's life, and he hadn't pressed, hadn't been remotely interested, cynically

deciding that any male Izzy Makepeace pro-
fessed to be in love with had to be loaded, and
that clearly the English guy had seen through
her and given her the elbow—hence her
removal to hunting pastures new.

But he knew differently now. She wasn't the
avaricious slapper he had named her. She had
loved the English guy. Still loved him.

He forced himself to unclench his jaw. As she
had said, it was none of his business. So why did
the pretty certain knowledge that Izzy would
regret her impetuosity and return to her lover, or
that he, like any red-blooded male, would track
her down and claim her leave him feeling so sour?

Change the subject.

Cool, impersonal tone.

He didn't do staff interviews. His personnel
officer handled that. But he'd give it his best
shot. It couldn't be too difficult.

'Having seen how you so brilliantly trans-
formed the grotty hovel that was Miguel's
home under his unlamented former house-

keeper's tenure, I would say your talents lie with the domestic.'

'Talents?' In spite of herself, Izzy went bright pink with pleasure. 'No one's ever linked that word with me before,' she confessed. Praise coming from this elevated being would be pretty rare, and she knew she would always treasure it—which was horribly feeble, and a rather shameful fact that wild horses wouldn't drag from her.

His heart, never the mushiest of organs, seemed to swell with sympathy. He recalled, now, something Miguel had said, that he'd ignored as would-be heart-tugging propaganda.

'Reading between the lines, I'd say her family treated her appallingly. Forever comparing her unfavourably with her brother, making her feel third-rate.'

'I believe you lived in the shadow of your brother, but that doesn't mean you don't have your own strengths. Different, but equal,' he remarked gently.

That brought her head up, and a slight frown to mar the smooth perfection of her brow. Miguel had certainly been giving his tongue full rein! She shrugged, a slight, defeated gesture.

Quite unaccountably, it moved him to say, 'You must have felt unloved. A lonely feeling, as I know. I was six years old when I overheard my father tell Tio Miguel, "If you feel so strongly, you spend time with the *mocoso*. By being born he cost me my adored wife's life. I'll see that my staff feed and clothe him, and he will be educated, but other than that I want nothing to do with him!"' His eyes hardened at the memory, but his voice was still gentle as he admitted, 'Until then I had tried every way I knew to make Papà notice me, love me. After that I stopped trying. I made my own life—with Tio Miguel to guide me when he was around.'

Appalled, Izzy opened her eyes very wide. They flooded with over-emotional tears. What a terrible thing for a lonely, motherless little boy to overhear! Her own nagged-at childhood didn't come near such a truly dreadful trauma.

A frown scoring his brow, Cayo managed to stop his fingers from brushing away the silvery teardrops. 'I'm not looking for sympathy,' he denied shortly, genuinely perplexed by the way he'd opened up to her. He had never repeated what he'd overheard to a living soul—not even Tio Miguel. In fact he hadn't even hung around to hear his uncle's response, he remembered, just run to the stables and sobbed himself to sleep. It was not an episode he had ever wished to talk about. So he didn't understand himself, and thoroughly loathed that state of affairs.

'I am merely pointing out that, regardless of what others might think of you, you do have talents and it's up to you to make something of your life. As I have done,' he proffered on a bite.

Make something of her life—as he had done? Thanks, but no thanks! Her tender heart twisted. Sure, he was a massively successful, wildly wealthy business tycoon, but apart from his uncle he cared for no one. Not even his gloriously beautiful mistresses, whom Miguel had unguardedly described as 'unemotional business arrangements'. His harsh, unloving father had been responsible for turning his son into a stranger to emotion, and that, in her book, made Cayo Angel Garcia a desperately poor man.

And she knew in that moment that she loved him.

Blinking back the annoyance of fresh tears, her heart hurting, she reached out a hand and touched the side of his extravagantly handsome face in an instinctive gesture of compassion.

She heard the catch of his breath. And then his lean, finely boned hands cupped her face, his long fingers splaying in her hair as he brought his dark head down to hers, his lips claiming hers with scorching demand, sending rivers of fire right down to her toes. The level of response she gave back to him as she greedily accepted the plundering of his tongue shocked her by its wild intensity.

His hands were on either side of her head, their hungry lips the only point of contact, and Izzy whimpered deep in her throat with the driving need for so very much more. She found her hands splayed against the breadth of his chest, touching him, and the erotic heat of him sent her out of her mind with need, with craving, with love…

CHAPTER TEN

THE COOL mountain breeze gave welcome relief from the midday heat that was baking the inner courtyard. But out here, beyond the massive castle walls, it danced amongst the high meadow flowers and carried the refreshing scent of pine. And if she closed her eyes Izzy was sure she could smell the sea which, so Miguel had told her, lay beyond the crumpled mountains of western Andalucia.

Dominating the limestone plateau, Las Palomas had to be the most beautiful place in the whole of Spain, Izzy decided as she watched Benji chase his tail in the long seeding grasses.

The little dog had improved almost beyond recognition since she'd found him cowering in that Madrid doorway. His once pitifully thin body was growing strong and sturdy, the mangy coat thicker and sleeker.

Izzy's smile was wistful.

The only opportunity she had to spend quality time with the rescued stray now was when she brought him out here to use up some of his boundless energy. The rest of the time he stuck to Miguel closer than Velcro. It was amazing how the pup and the elderly man had taken one look at each other and formed an immediate mutual admiration society.

Once, only half joking, she had told Miguel, 'Know something? I'm really jealous! The way Benji's taken to you puts my nose right out of joint!'

The elderly man had simply said, 'Look on the mutual devotion as a bonus. If you insist on leaving me and this beautiful place, and if Cayo insists on finding you paid employment—I guess it will be something truly exciting, like chambermaiding and a nice little room in an attic, if any of his hotels have attics, that is—then you will be pleased to know that your little stray has a happy and secure home here with me. Because, you see, my nephew was right. He always is, of course—and woe betide anyone who tries to tell him differently! I've decided to stay here permanently.'

That was the sensible way of looking at the situation, Izzy knew. Stupid to feel hurt because on learning of her decision to give up her job as his totally unnecessary companion her old gentleman had merely raised one brow, smiled what she had privately thought a suspiciously secret sort of smile and said, 'I see.' Not once had he tried to persuade her to change her mind. And there'd been a marked touch of unusual sarcasm in his voice when he'd mentioned chambermaiding and attics in the same breath!

Stupid to feel hurt. So she wouldn't. She would be sensible. Just as sensible as she'd been ever since Cayo had brought her back to Las Palomas five days ago. Then disappeared.

'Business,' Miguel had said, waving a languid, dismissive hand. 'The man doesn't know how to relax. But he'll be back for the Summer Ball.'

Which was today.

A huge marquee had been erected on one of the fastidiously tended sweeping lawns, and there tenant farmers and the inhabitants of the two sleepy villages which formed part of the vast Las Palomas property would be entertained with flamenco, dancing to a string quartet, and enough food and drink to keep an army going for a month.

Strings of coloured lights festooned the castle walls and every tree and fountain, just waiting for darkness to fall. The kitchens were a hive of activity as the chef and his helpers started preparing the banquet for the company of VIP guests and their wives and partners, who would apparently be arriving any time now to stay overnight, because she'd heard that the dancing would go on until dawn.

And there was still no sign of Cayo.

She chewed on a corner of her lower lip as she watched Benji chase a butterfly. She was being sensible about the future, and her departure from this lovely place, so she could congratulate herself. She was being adult about what had happened, too, she decided, feeling glum.

She'd fallen in love with Cayo—which was a silly thing to do, but she wasn't going to let herself obsess about it. Of course not. She'd get over it, given time. And so what if that kiss had given her a taste of rapture she was sure she would never experience again? She'd get over that, too. Maybe even forget it had ever happened.

Given time.

And time was what she'd had ever since he'd disappeared without so much as a, *see you*.

Time to think. About the way he'd broken that kiss as cataclysmically as he'd started it. Stepping away from her. Apologising! Looking as stiff and granite-faced as a carved effigy before snapping round on his heels and stalking away. Leaving her shuddering with the aftermath of exquisite physical sensation and the earth-shattering revelation of having fallen head over heels in love.

Lunch had been served in the sitting room of her suite that day, and he'd acted as though nothing had happened. The perfect, ultraconsiderate gentleman. She'd been disorientated by his annoying behaviour—she'd so wanted him to kiss her again, and he had behaved as if she were a kid sister, leaving her wanting to jump up and slap him. And all of that had been mixed up with the truly awesome bombshell of really falling in love, ensuring that she'd gone along with every last one of his suggestions.

That she allow him to show her something of the city, as formerly arranged. That Miguel's gift of the Fornier wardrobe be accepted, and that she spend some time at Las Palomas with his uncle while he sorted out a suitable occupation and affordable accommodation for her.

All commendably sensible.

And during the days that had followed, as he'd escorted her around Madrid's highspots, he had been the perfect companion—knowledgeable, kind, considerate. Only once, when he'd announced that they'd be dining out and going on to some classy-sounding nightclub, and she'd worn a silky little scarlet Fornier creation, had he taken one glance in her direction and looked as pained as if a hornet had taken a bite out of him. It had left her agonising over whether he'd looked like that because she looked tarty, wondering if the clinging dress was too short, showing too much cleavage to be acceptable in polite society.

She'd noticed that he hadn't really looked at her again, and when they'd hit the nightclub he'd suggested they leave almost immediately. He hadn't said one word to her on the short drive back to the hotel.

But apart from that Cayo's behaviour couldn't be faulted. So why had she swung between feeling dizzy with love for him and feeling so frustrated and miserable she could have screamed?

He had to be deeply ashamed of having kissed her, really regretted it, and was horrified by her more than merely enthusiastic response, she decided. She was deeply mortified as she recalled the way she had clung, squirmed and wriggled against his hard, lean body, as if she could never get close enough until she'd fused their bodies together.

Her hands had taken on a life of their own, touching, revelling in the strongly boned and muscled breadth of his shoulders, the smooth outline of his body where it narrowed to his taut, flat waist, and then moving up again like a heat-seeking missile so that her fingers could tangle in the midnight softness of his hair.

Her face flaming scarlet with humiliation, Izzy busied herself searching for Benji's favourite ball. She'd behaved like a real hussy. No wonder a guy as coolly sophisticated as Cayo had been turned off. If she wanted to do herself a favour she'd do as he had obviously done and put it out of her mind.

Right out.

Because…

Because just possibly there was something entirely different going on here. Suppose kissing her had been part of his plan? That he'd had to really steel himself to do it, and hadn't been able to bring himself to repeat it?

That possible scenario had occurred to her in the small hours of the night, waking her from a dream she'd been having of the first time he'd taken her hands in his.

He'd been apologising for thinking the worst of her, explaining that he had just that morning spoken to her former employer and had the truth from him regarding what had happened, confirming that she'd been blameless.

And all the time she'd been under the impression that he'd believed her side of the story when she'd recounted it much earlier. That impression had been strengthened when he'd immediately started to treat her like a human being—even to the extent of inviting her to accompany him to Madrid for a short holiday. So why, obviously still convinced that she was out to wriggle herself into Miguel's affections, to make herself indispensable and get her hands on his money, had he stopped calling her vile names, threatening her, and started being nice to her?

Her lush mouth wobbled now, as the only viable and most distressing answer that had presented itself in the small hours claimed residential status in her mind.

Miguel's wealth. Which Cayo would inherit. Provided the elderly man didn't marry, or leave it to a sneaky little gold-digger.

To make sure that didn't happen Cayo would have put himself up as a sort of well-heeled diversion, that would make the calculating heart of a career gold-digger beat faster and swiftly change allegiance.

He'd gritted his enviably strong white teeth, taken her hands in his, and acted as if he cared about her. Even kissed her silly to make her think he was more than a little attracted to her. And all the while not trusting her an inch—even though he'd claimed to have had the truth of her innocence from the horse's mouth.

He wouldn't believe in her innocence if the Angel Gabriel himself proclaimed it!

Despising herself for being so slow on the uptake, and falling for a man capable of such devious behaviour, she finally located the gaudy yellow and scarlet ball. She straightened, whistled for Benji, and threw it as far as she could over the tall grasses, watching as the puppy, yelping with excitement, scampered after it. And resolutely blinked the tears from her eyes.

'She is exercising our puppy.' Miguel laid aside the magnifying glass through which he'd been examining an illuminated manuscript and smiled as he answered his nephew's query. 'I believe she takes him beyond the immediate grounds and into the meadows, where he can run wild. You will find her if you look.'

He bit back a chuckle as he encountered the younger man's stony gaze and added, with seeming innocence, 'She will be pleased to see you. I believe she has missed you. She has been *desanimada*, without her usual sunny spirits.'

Deciding he'd said enough on that subject as Cayo's expression darkened, he probed slyly, 'Did you find alternative employment for my soon to be ex little companion?'

'Nothing suitable.' Cayo swung on his heels and exited, his strong, blue-shadowed jaw set at an uncompromising angle. Was his uncle trying to make him feel guilty?

He felt guilty enough without any input from him!

He had kissed her because he hadn't been able to stop himself. His legendary cool had deserted him. His mind, normally as reliable as a calculating machine, had seriously malfunctioned.

Punching a balled fist into the open palm of

his other hand, he left the castle by a rarely used side door, to avoid the interminable to-ings and fro-ings of his staff, and took a winding path that led towards the perimeter wall.

He had kissed Izzy and her response had sent what little had been left of his mind hurtling into orbit. The lush perfection of her body had pressed against his with an urgency she hadn't tried to hide, making the imperative to strip away the light barrier of clothes that separated them and make love to her a mere millimetre away from being acceded to.

Only his honour had stopped him in his tracks.

There was the type of women one married. Open, innocent, a little naïve perhaps. Good women. And Izzy, he now strongly suspected, fell into that category. As a confirmed bachelor—with no intention of marrying, not even for dynastic reasons—he avoided women such as these like the plague. There were other women widely available to more than satisfy his physical needs without troubling his conscience.

Beautiful, sophisticated, superficial and knowing women. Totally satisfied with the prospect of a handsome gift at the end of an invariably short and mutually advantageous affair.

Initially he had believed Izzy was another, more dangerous type. The type of woman who would latch on to any wealthy man and bleed him dry. He knew differently now, of course, which was why honour demanded he make full reparation. And keep his lustful thoughts and impulses to himself!

And that was why he was being drawn towards the meadows beyond the perimeter wall, he reasoned. To explain why he had so far failed in his duty to see that she didn't suffer from the loss of her job.

If his enquiries amongst his various personnel officers had raised eyebrows he had disregarded them. Izzy's placement would need to be special. He owed her. Which was why the job of cleaner at his Cadiz offices had been an outrageous suggestion, causing him in a moment of unfair anger to mentally mark down the man offering the available job for instant dismissal. Thankfully it had been a smothered reaction but it had only been topped by his withering scorn when he had been informed that there were openings for kitchen staff and waitresses in a couple of his hotels.

Even a position as an English-speaking trainee receptionist at his latest acquisition, a luxury hotel in Rome, had been deemed not good enough. Not for Izzy. She couldn't make herself understood in Spanish, in spite of the phrase-book which he'd noticed went everywhere with her. How she would manage in Italy was something he couldn't consider without a shudder.

The low wooden door that gave access to the open meadow land creaked as he opened it. Unless Izzy chose to return the long way round—across the fields and the horse paddocks, opening and closing several gates until she hit the long and steep approach road to the castle—she would return this way.

Shielding his eyes from the sun's glare, he scanned the meadow. And saw her. His heart flipped in his deep chest. Her silvery hair was piled in a haphazard mass on top of her head, and she was wearing a pair of lemon-yellow cotton shorts that clipped her curvy hips and displayed those shapely, lightly tanned legs to perfection. These were topped by a well worn and faded skimpy blue T-shirt that clung with loving softness to the enticing swell of her breasts.

And he ached to possess her. To discover, taste, own every last delicious inch of her.

Ignoring his fierce arousal, he clenched his fists at his sides as she approached, the dog dancing at her heels. Her steps slowed when she saw him. Judging by the way she was dressed the Fornier casuals were still languishing in their classy boxes. But she could wear a bin liner and still look delectable, he thought. She was that rarity: a woman who didn't need fancy clothes to make a stunning impact.

Recalling the night she'd worn that scarlet

designer gown, he smothered a groan. She had looked sensational. So ravishingly tempting he'd had to use every last ounce of his increasingly shaky self-control to stop himself from seducing her on the spot.

She stopped six feet away, her smile slight, uncertain. Her unadorned lips were the softest pink. They had tasted of heaven.

She was out of bounds. She wasn't the type to indulge in an affair and emerge unscathed. He would cut off his right hand before he caused her any hurt. And he certainly wasn't prepared to tie himself down in marriage just for the mental and physical relief of having her in his bed night after long, blissful night.

The reminder was unnecessary. His teeth clenched with brutal force.

He was glad of the diversion when the little dog hurtled towards him. Picking him up, holding the squirming body firmly while stoically enduring the welcoming slobbery doggy kisses, he reached a solution.

The only solution.

Setting the animal back on its feet, he straightened, and his voice was flat as he told her, 'As you know, I run a highly successful export business out of Cadiz. There are branch offices in the UK. There will be a job waiting for you there.' He'd insist on it. And when he insisted his staff turned themselves inside out to ensure his instructions were followed to the letter. 'Suitable accommodation will be found as part of the employment package.'

He named a salary that took her breath away. Her deep blue eyes widened until they seemed to fill her face. Something as cold and hard as a stone turned over inside her. She had come to love Spain—almost as much as she loved the man who stood before her, mantled in icy reserve. But she was to be packed off back to England.

It was for the best, she assured herself staunchly. She had fallen in love with a man who didn't know the meaning of the word. He had never known love as a child. His mother had died and his father had blamed him, turned his back on him. And, if her suspicions were correct, his intentions towards her were as devious as a pack of monkeys.

His intention had always been to get rid of her. Not quite with the flea in her ear, as he'd initially promised, but with a big fat bribe. Whoever had heard of an unqualified nobody commanding such a high salary, with free accommodation thrown in on top?

There was only one way his tricky mind would be working. He would have seen her demand that he bring her back here and her babbling about finding a job as a ploy to return to the gullible elderly man she'd been working on. Hence his swiftness in spiking her guns, by promising to find her suitable work and accommodation. It was all falling into place.

He hadn't been able to bring himself to carry out his intention to seduce her away from what he believed were her greedy designs on his naïve old uncle, because after that initial kiss the very thought of going further had turned his stomach. But he was still desperate to get her away from his wealthy beloved relative.

Her chin came up. He was so unfairly, incredibly handsome she didn't know whether to slap him or burst into tears.

She did neither. She could be tricky, too.

'Thanks for the offer. I might well take it. Or I might decide to stay on as your uncle's companion.' Completely out of the question, but he wasn't to know that. And the threat should give him a huge dose of indigestion! Her blue eyes sparked. 'I'll let you know.' And she walked away.

Cayo's eyes narrowed as he watched her. Part of him wanted to spank her. Part of him admired the way she always managed to stand up to him. And yet another part, the most insistent of all, wanted to make love to her until she didn't know where she was.

CHAPTER ELEVEN

PRE-DINNER drinks were being served by smoothly circulating white-coated waiters. In the main salon, beneath the breathtakingly beautiful painted ceiling, the A-list guests mingled. The noise level was muted, because these superbly groomed sophisticates didn't do rowdy, full-on partying. And the jewels displayed on pampered pale fingers, around elegant necks and pinned into glossy, expensively styled hair would probably pay off the national debt of any large third-world country.

Izzy shivered. She *so* didn't want to be here.

The sore thumb.

People were looking at her—not ill-bred enough to stare, of course, but sending ever so slightly inquisitive looks in her direction, as if she were a gatecrasher, muscling in where she had no right to be. And it wasn't as if she'd appeared in her oldest jeans and shrunken jumper, either.

The classy floor-length Fornier creation in soft ice-blue satin either skimmed or clung in all the right places, and she'd taken endless pains to anchor her hair securely on top of her head. It was far too early on in the evening for it to be doing its own thing and tumbling all over the place.

Clutching her untouched flute of champagne, she wished she'd stuck to her guns and taken herself off for an early night. But Miguel had made her promise.

She'd spent the late afternoon with him and the tenants, mixing and mingling, entranced by the flamenco display, clapping along with everyone else, and reduced to helpless giggles when she and the fat farmer who'd invited her to dance had fallen over each other's feet. He'd sat on the grass, legs outsplayed, roaring with laughter, and a small crowd had gathered and started clapping and cheering.

She guessed she was good at making a fool of herself, if nothing else! But it had all been good fun, and when Miguel had announced his intention of retiring and skipping the later, more sophisticated banquet and ball, she'd said she'd do the same. But…

'I can plead age and infirmity. And disinclination. You can do no such thing. And you will enjoy it. I want you to promise me you'll attend. To please me? Cayo will look after you.'

But Cayo was doing no such thing. Looking head and shoulders more handsome and charismatic than any other guy in the room, he was circulating, his smile effortlessly charming, the white dinner jacket he was wearing making him look good enough to eat.

Ignoring her.

She sighed. Telling porkies—saying she might after all stay on as Miguel's companion, thus getting her own back on Cayo for his hard-headed intention to get rid of her, get her right out of the country—didn't seem such a brilliant idea right now.

The moment he could drag himself away from the flirtatious Spanish beauty dressed in black and wearing enough diamonds to sink a battleship, she would dive in, tell him she would accept the job back home and leave Spain as soon as it could be arranged. Then she would go to her room with all speed.

And she would never see him again—because she would lose no time, once back in England, in looking for something else—anything. Because he might at some time in the future make a flying visit to the UK office, and she didn't want to be there when he did. It would set her back miles and miles on the road to recovering from her ill-conceived love for the brute.

Itching to act on that decision, she was more dismayed than puzzled when the butler silently advanced on her and told her she had a visitor.

'In the great hall, *señorita*. He is waiting. He says he is your brother.'

Jettisoning her unwanted drink on a convenient table, Izzy hitched up her narrow silk skirts and tottered on the highest heels Madame Fornier had provided after the gliding butler.

What on earth could James be doing here? Half a world away from his important work, the home she'd been told was the last word in refinement, and his clever, sensible wife—all the things that boosted his overblown ego.

Trust him to turn up when she least wanted to see him! He was her brilliant big brother, and she admired him, but he could be a real pain. Like the time when she'd been around eight and he'd found her experimenting with their mother's make-up. Lipstick and mascara, rouge and eyeshadow had been daubed in great clown-like splodges, when she should have been in her own room, as instructed, copying out a list of the kings and queens of England, complete with dates and fates, in her best handwriting.

He'd sneaked on her—of course he had—and got her into boiling hot water! Metaphorically and literally. Her father had grabbed her by the scruff of her neck and scrubbed her face with soap and hot water, and her mother had vented one of her long-suffering, despairing sighs and rushed to try to rescue what she could of her ruined cosmetics.

Now James was here. And she had no idea how or why. Tall, thin, with a long face and light brown hair thinning on top, he looked a decade older than forty. He was like a stark accusation in the perfumed frivolity of the enormous flower-decked space. 'What on earth are you doing here?' she said bluntly.

'Fetching you home,' he snapped back at her. 'When we received your letter breaking the news that you'd left your job as mother's help, and were working for an old man you'd apparently met in some backstreet, we had a family meeting and decided unanimously that you had to be brought away. Either to New Zealand, where we can keep an eye on what you're doing, or more usefully back to the job in Father's old practice you so stupidly left.'

His long features were flushed with barely controlled anger. His precious dignity must be precariously balanced, Izzy guessed. He would be feeling uncomfortable and stupid—an effect he and, to a slightly lesser degree, her parents had always had on *her*.

'Father's spoken to the new head of practice and he's willing—with certain reservations, naturally—to give you your job back.' He glowered his impatience. 'Do you have any idea how much time I'm wasting on your behalf? How much inconvenience I've been put to? Travelling halfway round the world to drum some sense into your head! You weren't at the address you'd given, but a neighbour told me where you'd gone, and with whom. That you've foisted yourself on the charity of a family of such high social and financial standing leaves me appalled and practically speechless. You've been a nuisance and a dis-appointment since the day you were born, but this takes the biscuit!'

Izzy cut off her self-destructive impulse to point out that he didn't *sound* speechless, because she knew from unpleasant past experience that answering James back brought swift and usually painful retribution.

'I haven't foisted myself on anyone—' Izzy did her best to defend herself, but her voice was thick with tears. James always made her feel a no-account failure, and he obviously wasn't going to listen to a word she said.

'I have a taxi waiting and our flights back to the UK leave first thing in the morning,' he cut in coldly. 'So I'd appreciate it if you'd pack your things and be quick about it while I find Señor Garcia and apologise on your behalf.'

'No apologies are necessary.' Cayo strode forward. He'd heard enough. If he heard any more he'd take that long streak of disdain by the scruff of his neck and throw him off his property.

Izzy's bright head was bent, her slender shoulders sagging with humiliation. Anger on her behalf boiled inside him. So this was the brilliant brother who'd always cast such a shadow over her, causing odious comparisons—and being made to feel third-rate, as Miguel had suspected—and blighting her young life.

His mouth tightened in unforgiving lines as, reaching her side, he slid an arm around her tiny waist. He felt her tremble, saw her eyes sweep up to seek his—deepest blue, glittering with unshed tears. Tears of humiliation.

His hand tightened protectively around her. She leaned into him. And his voice was flint, his eyes even harder, as he informed the older man, 'Izzy stays here for precisely as long as she is happy to. She is my welcome guest.' His accent thickened. 'Should I ever hear you speaking like that to her again you will find your teeth at the back of your throat.'

Seeing James Makepeace, brilliant surgeon,

turn the colour of an overripe tomato gave him immense satisfaction—although it shouldn't, of course. He had never threatened anyone with physical violence before, or been so deliberately, bluntly rude. He'd always regarded such behaviour as being uncouth. And uncouth he wasn't. Chilling politeness when displeased was more his style. But something about this situation had made him lose his cool. Big-time.

Carefully moderating his tone, reining in his astonishing pugilistic impulses, he imparted, with the calm of a frozen lake, 'Your sister is among friends who value her, who will care for her. I suggest you relay *that* information to your parents.'

Izzy could hardly believe her ears! Or her eyes! Cayo had leapt to her defence! He must have followed her out, heard the bulk of what had been said and waded in to put her brother firmly in his place. Something that, to her knowledge, had never happened to him before. He was more used to being spoiled, praised and listened to as if he were the fount of all wisdom. And now James, who always gave the impression of being vastly superior to anyone in his vicinity, was looking distinctly uncomfortable.

Her soft heart melted. He was her brother, after all. And if he'd come looking for her because he cared for her, was worried for her, then she would have done as he'd said—packed her things and left with him. As it was, all he'd done was make her feel she was a nuisance, that her behaviour in attaching her useless self to such an important family was shameworthy enough to warrant a man-to-man apology.

A lump in her throat, she offered, 'James— I'm really sorry you felt you had to come all this way. There was no need, truly. And tell Dad I'll pass on going back to the practice.' The thought of returning to her one-time work place, where everyone would know of her juvenile crush on Marcus, would be laughing at the way she'd run errands for him, cleaned his flat just for a kind word, made her feel queasy. 'Because Señor Garcia has offered me a job in his UK offices. As soon as I take that up I'll phone and let you know.'

At her side she felt Cayo's lean, muscled body stiffen. Relief because he'd soon see the back of her? Because she wasn't going to do as she'd threatened and stay on for ever as Miguel's totally unnecessary companion with the aim of getting her hands on his wealth as was his impossible-to-shift conviction?

But that didn't fit with the way his arm still curved protectively around her tense body, the way he'd leapt to defend her against James's cutting tongue. Unless he was the type of guy who always took the underdog's side, deserving or not…

She raised a shaky hand to rub at the crease of bewildered confusion between her eyes, and heard Cayo's stiffly polite tones as he offered, 'May we give you some refreshment before you leave?' She looked up to catch her brother's tight-lipped, disapproving expression before he uttered a brief negative, turned and walked out. Not deigning to comment on the new job, not even looking at her. Not saying goodbye.

Tears flooded her eyes. She was ashamed of the weakness. She'd always known her family didn't rate her—and James in particular—so she shouldn't let what had happened upset her so much.

Cayo dropped his arm from her waist. Her body felt icy cold where his touch had been. His voice rough with unconcealed humour, he told her, 'I do believe your very proper brother thinks I'm keeping you here as my paramour, *querida*!'

Izzy's breasts heaved and a hot knot of misery rose in her throat. The idea of being his paramour made her legs go weak, took her breath away, but *he* found it unthinkable enough to be amusing!

And he had probably guessed James's suspicions correctly. After all, Cayo had been very defensive of her—standing up close, sliding his arm around her, proprietorial and protective.

And how many times in the past had James accused her of being a brainless blond bimbo? Dozens! Brainless enough to shack up with the first man to ask her?

She shivered. The guests would be being ushered through to be seated at the enormous dining table any time now, to enjoy the sumptuous banquet the chef and his assistants had been preparing all day. She wouldn't be among their number. She had to hole up somewhere quiet, where she could think, try to assess this latest situation, try to work out what Cayo really thought about her.

'You are upset.' Strong hands fastened on her naked shoulders, turning her into him. 'Look at me.'

Hardly daring to, because this close to him it was impossible not to look up into those lean, bronzed features, impossible to slap down the absolute and terrifying need to reach up and cover that charismatically handsome face with fevered, desperate kisses. But he lifted a hand,

and the feel of the pads of his long fingers just beneath her chin had her raising her eyes to his, willpower flying.

A tear escaped, trembled on her lashes and fell. He bent his dark head and captured it with his lips. 'Please don't cry. He's not worth it.'

Cayo had never considered the position of his heart before. It functioned. End of story. But now he definitely felt that reliable organ make itself known, turning to warm, soft marshmallow. A deep breath tugged at his lungs.

He knew exactly what it felt like to grow up without knowing love. Izzy had had her family around her, but all they had done, apparently, was compare her unfavourably with her brainy big brother and make her feel unimportant, a nuisance, a total failure, because she didn't match her brother's brilliant achievements. And she hadn't had a kindly, caring uncle to make her feel valued, as he had.

'You are ten times the human being your brother is. From the little I've seen of him, and heard, he's a cold, pompous, insensitive prig—he may be a clever surgeon, but you are warm, feisty, and you give of yourself. Remember that.'

His voice was so low it was almost a whisper, and Izzy gasped as he swung her into his arms. Still reeling from the light, lingering touch of his lips on the angle of her cheekbone, she could only cling on for dear life as he skirted the newly erected dais where the mini-orchestra would play for those who wished to dance later and effortlessly mounted the ancient stone staircase.

Reaching the room she was using, he slid her to her feet, slid her down the length of his body, shattering the small amount of equilibrium left to her. Her mind went blank, and she was stingingly aware of the heat pulsing through her, pooling deep in her tummy, of the way her unbearably sensitised breasts pushed against the pale blue satin.

Desperately hanging on to the very last scrap of sanity left to her, she turned—turned her back to him. The unpleasant scene with James was forgotten, unimportant. The only feeling to possess her mind, soul and body was her self-destructive love for this urbane, tricky, devastatingly charismatic man, who could have his pick of the world's most beautiful and suitable females.

She should be locked up for her own protection!

'You should go now. Your guests will be missing you.' Her voice was shaking so much she wondered how she'd managed to get the words out.

'Let them. Iglesias—' he named his butler '—is discreet and intelligent, which is why he holds his position here. He will see the banquet runs smoothly without my presence.'

Cayo's brooding eyes caressed the nape of her neck. Pale and vulnerable. One of the shoe-string straps had dropped, now lay across the smooth warm flesh of her upper arm. The line of her shoulder and neck was exquisite. His fingers itched to remove the pins that restricted the gloriously untamed tangle of silky silvery curls so he could bury his face in its perfumed softness. She smelled evocatively of sunshine, fresh air and flowers.

Hadn't anyone, at any time, told her how beautiful she was? How special?

He could fully understand now why his uncle was so fond of her, so protective. A sensitive and wise man, he had seen the intrinsic goodness of her caring nature—where he had seen only a devious schemer, believing he was right until Augustin del Amo had admitted the truth.

He should be hung, drawn and quartered— along with her wretched family for their collective criminal blindness. And the idea that manufacturing a job for her in the UK was adequate recompense for his initial behaviour towards her made him cringe with shame.

His body hardened unbearably. He gave a silent groan. He wanted this woman with an urgency he had never fully experienced before.

Therefore, and entirely logically… 'Izzy.' He placed large hands on her slender shoulders and turned her to face him. 'Marry me.'

CHAPTER TWELVE

IN TOTAL tongue-tying shock, Izzy could only stare up into his heartstoppingly beautiful features, her eyes widening until they almost filled her delicate, furiously colouring face. Had she finally lost all of her sanity? Every last, dwindling scrap of it!

Perhaps it was the overwhelming, vital force of the closeness of his lean and fantastic body, the bone-dissolving touch of his hand on her over-sensitised skin. Or maybe it was the headily seductive perfume of the many deep bowls of ghostly white lilies, coupled with the witchy dark shadows that were creeping from the corners of the timelessly elegant room, that had spooked her into totally losing her grip on reality.

She shook her head sharply in a vain attempt to clear it. She felt the mass of her hair start to tumble, and wished he'd move away, stop touching her. And then, chaotically, she wished he'd move even closer.

'Well, *amada*?' Cayo murmured, soft and only just audible, his hands moving to gently cradle her face, his fingers splayed in the silken blond glory of her hair.

He was too bewitched by her brilliant eyes, the slightly trembling, luscious pink and temptingly kissable mouth, to ask himself why a man who had vowed never to marry should do the absolutely unthinkable and shackle himself, while of sound mind, to one woman. A woman who would have the right to make demands on his time, his privacy, his valued independence. But moments ago he had opened his mouth and listened to a proposal come out.

'Sorry.' It was a gigantic effort to speak at all. Scrambling frantically for some shred of down-to-earth reality, Izzy said, 'I guess I didn't hear you too well.' Her voice wobbled disgracefully. He couldn't really have asked her to marry him, could he? Him? It was so unlikely it made her feel really weird.

The pad of one thumb trailed delicately over her parted lips. The other tucked beneath her chin, positioning her mouth beneath his, and his voice was thick as he repeated, 'Marry me, *amada.*' Lowering his head slowly until his lips were a whisper away from the trembling, agonising expectancy of hers, he said, 'Say yes, my Isabella.' Light as silk, soft and warm as melted honey, his mouth touched hers, breathing the imperative deep into her soul. 'Say it. Say yes.'

Reduced to a shivering, clinging mass of dizzy, shameless longing, she breathed her answering mindless affirmative—and gasped with excruciating excitement as he claimed her mouth with unashamed masculine urgency. Her knees gave way beneath her as his tongue plunged with masterful sensuality deep into the moist sweetness of her mouth.

In answer to her suddenly boneless predicament, Cayo lifted her in his arms and carried her to the massive four-poster. Brushing aside the filmy white drapes, he laid her on the ivory silk counterpane, his fierce arousal disordering his breathing. Never before had he felt so hot for a woman, and it felt good—so good.

His body strained to claim hers, to plunge deeply into the hot slickness of her. But this had to be special. For the first time in his life he wanted to give pleasure more than he wanted to take it.

Bending to trail his fingers over her delicate collarbone, he vowed, 'I will make you happy, my Izzy.' He allowed his fingers to trail lower, over the tantalising upper swell of her breasts, until he came to the barrier of satin. He moved them slowly down, over the soft fabric, sucking in a deep breath as his hands cradled the glorious bounty of her breasts, registered the tormenting hardness of her straining nipples.

He breathed something rawly fractured in

his own language and then lifted her, his long sure fingers dealing with the back fastening of her dress.

Exultant, Izzy helped him. She loved Cayo with a depth that both shocked and delighted her, and she wanted him with an urgent need that broke the bounds of what she had dreamed possible. Hedonistically she gloried in her nakedness as the last scraps of silk and lace were removed and heedlessly tossed aside. And lay in the misty, bewitching dusk, watching as he dealt summarily with his own clothes, her eyes never leaving him, his eyes never leaving her.

Izzy squirmed impatiently with the flame of greedy excitement. He exuded raw sexual power. The breadth of his magnificent golden-skinned shoulders, the muscular strength of his deep chest, long powerful thighs. Responsive heat engulfed her.

This gorgeous, totally adored man wanted her as his wife!

She lifted welcoming arms as he took the single stride that brought him back to her and slid beside her. His voice was thick as he ground out, 'I've wanted you like this for far too long, *amada*. Every time I looked at you I wanted to take you to bed. Holding back has driven me half crazy!' And his mouth took hers again, with a passion that sent her deep into delirium.

Izzy came awake slowly. The sun was up, golden light spilling in bands over the luxurious carpet. Cradled in Cayo's arms, she stretched languorously and turned glowing eyes to him as he hoisted himself on one elbow, brushed the tangle of curls from her forehead and dropped a light kiss between her brows.

'*Buenos días, querida,*' he murmured, dark eyes soft and slumbrous. 'Last night was wonderful. All I ever dreamed it could be.'

Her thoughts precisely. Although 'wonderful' seemed an inadequate way to describe what had happened. Fantastic and earth-shattering hit the spot a little more accurately. Though what had happened between them during the night hours had been beyond any words at a mere mortal's command, she decided, feeling distinctly awestruck.

Wrapping her arms around him, she nuzzled into the warm solidity of his chest, a dreamy smile curving her lips as she pleaded softly, 'Tell me you love me?' She wanted to hear those words so badly—wanted to share what she felt with him.

For a moment he seemed to tense. She felt the tightening of the muscles in his back, and then he gave a soft laugh, spread her on her back. He lowered his lips to hers and promised, 'I love your mouth, your hair, your fantastically sexy body.'

He dipped a sure hand between her thighs and she had to fight to stop herself from screaming with ecstasy as he found the slick, pulsating seat of her sex, and stars exploded deep inside her as he proceeded to demonstrate exactly how much he loved her body.

* * *

'What are you doing?'

'Getting dressed.'

Well, that was obvious, Izzy thought as she came properly awake, peering at him through lazy, love-drenched eyes. A knot of unbelievable excitement clenched inside her. She was going to be his *wife*! Life simply couldn't get better than this!

Getting dressed… Pushing his dress shirt into the narrow waistband of his beautifully tailored black trousers.

Hoisting herself up against the pillows, she pushed her hair out of her eyes. She might be disappointed, but she wasn't going to show it. 'I had this fantasy of our having breakfast in bed together, and then the two of us having a nice little lie-in,' she confided lightly. Her eyes sparkled. She felt so comfortable with him now—part of him, almost. She could say anything, tease him.

But he wasn't smiling. Indolent dark eyes were fastened on the lushly full globes of her naked breasts, and a muscle at the side of his sensual mouth tightened. 'It is a fantasy I wish I could enjoy, *querida.*' He came to her, touched his lips to each pink crest in turn, and then to her mouth.

Izzy sighed voluptuously, her hands going to his flat waist, tugging him towards her. Would she ever be able to get enough of him? She didn't think so! She had never dreamed such passion could exist.

But he took her hands, laid them at her sides and tucked the sheet up to her chin. 'Don't tempt me,' he growled, but he was smiling. And then he was serious as he told her, 'I want you to promise to say nothing of our betrothal for now—not even to Miguel. In a few days, when your brother has had time to get back to his home and is calmer, we will phone and break the news—invite him, his wife and your parents to our wedding. James and I didn't part on the best of terms,' he understated. 'For your sake I would like things to be on a happier footing. To that end, you must be able to truthfully tell your family that they are the first to hear of our plans.'

He straightened, ruffling his fingers through her hair. 'While I'm anxious for my uncle to share our good news, I really do believe that under the circumstances your family should be the first to know. That is why I don't want any member of my staff to discover me sharing your room. The gossip would spread around the castle like wildfire, and Miguel would be morally outraged if he thought I was taking advantage of you! So until we can break the news to your family it must be our secret. Besides, I need to personally apologise to James for my less than welcoming behaviour—I would hate to cause a rift between our families.'

He grinned disarmingly, running his fingers through his already rumpled midnight hair, and Izzy smiled back. Loving him. It was really good of him to want her family to feel special because they were to be the first to be told of her forthcoming marriage.

Watching him collect last night's discarded white dinner jacket before leaving the room, Izzy felt her heart nearly burst with love. He was such a diplomat! For her sake he would actually apologise to her pompous, ultra-critical brother, and maybe her whole family would for once change their entrenched opinions and admit that in falling in love with Cayo Garcia she hadn't been so stupid, after all!

The stout castle walls seemed to hum with activity when Izzy finally left her room, dressed in a cool cotton skirt and a pretty cropped top—courtesy of Madame Fornier's excellent taste.

Staff were clearing away all signs of last night's festivities and dealing with the after-math of the buffet breakfast that had apparently been served. Her stomach rumbled—a reminder that she hadn't eaten in ages.

Cayo, casually dressed in cream-coloured chinos and a crisp shirt, was overseeing the exodus of the overnighting guests. Wondering if he was making his excuses for having missed the banquet, or if he was sticking to the alpha male's creed of never explaining, never apologising, she grinned wickedly and headed for the kitchens.

Rodolfo, the chef's assistant, was feeding Benji. He looked up and grinned widely. '*Señorita*, may I get you something? Coffee, perhaps? Or maybe—' he put a doleful expression on his boyish face '—you only come to take this hairy one for the walk?'

Every time she encountered Rodolfo he pretended to try to flirt with her—a habit that would vanish once he learned she was to marry his master. She grinned right back at him. This morning she wanted to smile at everyone. 'Coffee would be lovely.'

Spying a tray of crusty rolls—left over from breakfast service, she guessed—she helped herself. She bit gratefully into the crisp crust and wondered if she would be able to catch Cayo after the last of the guests had left. She knew she would have to avoid Miguel for the rest of the day, because he would be sure to ask how she had enjoyed the ball he'd been so insistent she attended.

Give him twenty-four hours and he would, as usual, be so lost in his work he would have forgotten all about it. Sipping gratefully at the coffee Rodolfo gave her, she watched Benji finish his breakfast and chase his empty bowl over the slabbed floor. She tried to imagine her wedding dress—sleek, sophisticated silk, or frothy in-your-face bridal lace? Picturing herself in either, walking up the aisle on her father's arm to Cayo, who would look devastatingly handsome, made her stomach twist itself into knots.

Unable to stand still a moment longer, she smiled beatifically at nothing in particular, called to Benji and exited by the maze of corridors that brought her out into the service courtyard. She made her way to the perimeter meadows, where the puppy could run and play.

There she sat, in the long seeding grasses, and waited. Waited in a bone-melting, loving trance until Cayo joined her.

'I knew you'd find me.' Eyes sparkling, she gazed up at him with unhidden adoration, reached for his hand as he hunkered down beside her.

Brilliant dark eyes set within heavy black lashes gleamed at her. 'How could I not? Come.' He straightened, whistled for the puppy, who was chasing a bee with no chance of success, and pulled her to her feet. 'There are soft rugs and a large picnic hamper waiting for us in my car. I want you to myself,' he confided thickly. 'Today we find a remote mountain meadow and we make love until the stars shine above us. Do you want that as much as I do, *querida*?'

Want it? Izzy nodded vigorously. She felt as though she were floating in space, her bones and flesh turning to jelly at his words. She wanted him so much she could barely walk, let alone speak!

CHAPTER THIRTEEN

IZZY tucked the hem of a soft sage-green sleeveless blouse into the waistband of a cream-coloured linen skirt. It was surprising how she'd got used to wearing the sort of beautiful, classy clothes she wouldn't have dared to even look at, let alone been able to afford to buy in her previous permanently cash-strapped existence, she mused as she peered in the tall looking glass, trying to bring some semblance of order to her defiantly wayward hair.

The only thing she couldn't get used to was Cayo's absence.

He'd been away for five days, ten hours—she checked her watch—and thirty-five minutes.

She missed him so much that every fibre in

her body ached. Missed the nights when he had come to her room, the days spent well away from the castle, exploring the countryside, making love, eating in little out-of-the-way inns, returning late at night to make love again. Missed the sound of his voice, being able to look at him, drink in all that lean and magnificent male beauty.

It had been an idyll. So utterly perfect she'd felt mildly disorientated, as if she were living in a wonderful dream. Until…

'*Querida*, I have to be away for a day or so.'

Coming down for early breakfast one day—discreetly, arriving in the sunny garden room at a different time from him—she had found him swallowing the last of his coffee, dressed in a light grey designer suit and a pristine darker grey shirt. He had taken her breath away. 'I'm sorry, but something's come up that I can't deal with from here.' His dark eyes had been veiled. He hadn't looked at her. Getting to his feet, he had reached for the document case stowed beside his chair. 'I'll be back before you know it.'

Izzy had sat down with a bump.

Running down the massive staircase, dressed the way she knew he liked to see her, in a floaty flowered skirt topped by the bikini top he always said he couldn't resist removing the moment they were assured of privacy, she had been almost bouncing up and down in her impatience to phone her parents in Wellington and break the fantastic news of her forthcoming wedding.

'But it's been four days,' she reminded him in a breathy rush, 'James will be settled back home by now. I thought we could phone them this morning.' She angled a beaming smile at him. 'I can't wait to tell everyone!'

'It can wait for a day or two longer.' He dropped a distracted kiss on the top of her head, straightened, and prepared to leave.

Izzy caught his hand, preventing his departure, deeply disappointed by the further delay, and even more so by his planned absence. It drained all the joy out of her day, and she queried, 'When did you decide you had to leave?'

Disconcerted, he frowned, removing his hand from her clutching fingers. 'Last night. Does it matter?'

Last night—while they'd been making love? Had his mind been elsewhere, busily planning this morning's departure? She felt her face flush. 'But you said nothing,' she accused miserably. 'If I'd come down half an hour later would you just have left? Without a word?'

Unused to having his actions questioned by anyone, Cayo stifled a snappy response. Some creative thinking was called for here. But making excuses for his behaviour was beyond him. 'Don't be silly. Of course not!' A fleeting smile. 'Don't pick a fight, *querida*!'

Five minutes later, listening to the noise of helicopter rotors beat the air, Izzy felt abandoned and utterly miserable, like a commodity to be used when time allowed and then put aside, forgotten, when something more interesting popped over the horizon. He hadn't even bothered to warn her that he'd have to go away on business.

Then she told herself to grow up. Fast! She was to marry a man who controlled vast wealth, many highly successful business enterprises. Of course there would be times when he had to take off at the drop of a hat. What sort of wife would she make if she sniped at him or sulked whenever that happened?

The sort of wife he would soon wish he'd never met, she informed herself grimly.

So she would take his sudden departures, his obvious concentration on the work at hand, with good grace—accept that his air of abstraction, of distance from her, was because his mind was preoccupied with whatever business dealings lay ahead. She would make him a wife he could be proud of, and not act like a whining child suddenly deprived of its favourite toy!

Now, slipping her feet into low-heeled

pumps, she reflected uneasily that it had been almost two weeks since he'd asked her to marry him and it was still a secret.

A secret she was bursting to share!

Yesterday she'd been sorely tempted to phone her family and share the news that was lodged like a great heavy rock in her chest, bursting to get out. A temptation so strong she had found her hand resting on the phone on a couple of occasions.

But she had resisted, albeit with difficulty, and she congratulated herself thinly. Cayo had asked her to wait. He wanted to speak to her parents personally and make his apologies to James—smooth her brother's ruffled feathers, make sure no bad feeling existed between him and her family. So for his sake she'd grit her teeth and keep her impatience under wraps.

Satisfied that she looked reasonably calm and collected, she left her room to join Miguel for afternoon tea. She smiled softly, glad to have something to think of other than Cayo's frustratingly long absence.

It was a ritual the elderly man had insisted on since his nephew's sudden departure. English afternoon tea, complete with tiny triangular cucumber sandwiches and seed cake, was to be served at four every afternoon in the library.

She'd told him that the custom had virtually died out with the Edwardians, but he'd insisted, and always used the occasion to gently quiz her. Was she happy at Las Palomas? Did the heat of high summer make her miss her cooler home climes? And, more pertinently, was she missing the young man she'd left behind? Was she still hurting over him?

She longed, quite desperately, to confide that she and his nephew were to marry, that in the near future she'd be part of the family, and she had to bite her tongue to stop the words bubbling out in an excited torrent. She reminded herself that, nominally at least, she was still supposed to be here as Miguel's companion.

Wondering what gentle questions she would have to parry this afternoon, she approached the partly opened library door. And stopped in her tracks as she heard voices. Delighted colour flooded her cheeks, and her heart leapt wildly.

Cayo was back!

About to push the door fully open, wondering how she would be able to act normally, stop herself from flinging herself into his arms, she froze.

Because Cayo—her adored, soon-to-be-husband—was saying, 'On the subject of marriage, Tio, I have told you—a man would be a fool to settle for one flower when he can flit from one blossom to another with impunity and retain his freedom...'

Smothering a gasp as her heart lurched sickeningly, Izzy flattened herself against the wall for support, shutting out the excruciating sound of the words that spelled out her betrayal. How could he *say* those things? And sound so amused when saying them? How could he do that to her?

Unaware that her cheeks were wet with tears, she fled back to her room.

Her heart felt as if it had been split in two with a very sharp knife. He'd spelled it out, clear as spring water. He would use a woman when the urge hit him. Move on to the next when the challenge of pursuit was sated. Not caring who got hurt in the process so long as he kept his precious freedom!

Oh, how could he?

He'd had no intention of marrying her, she conceded bitterly. No wonder he'd been so insistent on keeping their phantom wedding plans secret!

Angry colour stung her cheekbones. What had he planned? To distance himself for a few days, thus giving her unashamed ardour time to cool—her face flamed anew at the reminder of just how unashamed she had proved to be—and then on his return calmly inform her that he'd changed his mind? There would be no wedding. He would resurrect the offer of a job in the UK and wave her goodbye at the airport without a flicker of conscience.

Because the high and mighty Cayo Angel Garcia didn't own such an uncomfortable thing!

Recalling how blown away she'd been when he'd confessed that he'd been wanting to get her into bed, had had difficulty holding back, she bared her teeth in a grimace of self-loathing.

She'd already been head over heels in love with him, and—naïve idiot, that she was—his offer of marriage had clinched it. She'd thrown herself body, heart and soul into bed with him. How he would have gloated! And now, having sated his sexual curiosity, he was preparing to ditch her.

Far too late she remembered how she'd been so suspicious of his motives between leaving Madrid and his sudden, out-of-the-blue proposal of marriage, wondering if his bewildering behaviour meant he didn't entirely believe the truth he'd said he'd had from Augustin del Amo. And the way he'd called her *querida*—his translation of the word paramour, which she knew was an outdated term for mistress. How could she have so brainlessly allowed her heart to rule what passed for her brains?

Her family were right.

She was a fool.

Her own worst enemy.

Everything she did crumbled to ignominious failure!

Now she had to decide what to do. Pacing the floor and grinding her teeth would get her nowhere.

Stay and face him? Tell him exactly what she thought of him?

Water off a duck's back.

Besides, she couldn't trust herself not to give herself away—let him see how very much she'd adored him, how the hurt he'd dealt her went so deep she didn't think she'd ever get over it. Such information would fuel his already massive ego. So, no thanks. Such an outpouring of condemnation might bring her temporary relief, but the consequences would be cringe-making, and she couldn't bear to let herself down to that extent.

Or go?

Simply go?

Let him think she'd ditched him before he got the chance to tell her she was history?

Right. As good as done. It was the only way she could hope to salvage something from this ghastly situation.

Flying to the escritoire, she dug out a sheet of headed notepaper, scrabbled for a pen and scrawled.

It was fun while it lasted, and thanks for your offer, but I'll pass.

As a further dig she added:

I'm afraid it would take more than you can offer to tempt me to give up my freedom.

She stuffed it into an envelope, and propped it against the bed pillows before she could change her mind. There was a tight ball of misery in her chest because the thought of marrying him had made her deliriously happy—happier than she'd ever been in her entire life.

Scrambling out of her skirt and blouse, she dragged on a pair of her old jeans and a crumpled T-shirt and pushed the rest of her gear into her rucksack. She would take nothing she hadn't arrived with.

Passport. Purse. Her hand hovered over the cheque Miguel had given her—to make up for the pitifully low wages he had unthinkingly paid her back in Cadiz, he'd told her as he'd pressed it into her hands. A cheque she had had no intention of ever cashing. Reluctantly slipping it into her passport, she closed the straps of her battered rucksack. She had to be practical, even though she felt like having hysterics and breaking things. She would need money to tide her over until she could find work, though she felt horribly uneasy over taking it.

Her mangled heart gave another painful lurch. She would miss her old gentleman, and hated to leave without saying goodbye, giving Benji one last cuddle. At least she was confident that Miguel would look after the little stray. She would write to him when she was settled somewhere. Tell him how fondly she remembered being his housekeeper in Cadiz, and that she would always remember him with affection. To seek him out now would involve making explanations of a sort—which he probably wouldn't believe because she couldn't tell him the truth. And she'd run the risk of bumping into Cayo.

The thought that even now she might not be able to avoid him brought her heart to her mouth. True, she could jump in before he had a chance to open his mouth and tell him she'd decided that no way could she marry him, thanks all the same. But she knew that she would have zero hope of doing that without giving her true feelings of hurt and betrayal away, dissolving into accusations and floods of shaming tears.

Taking a deep breath, she tried to reassure herself that Cayo wouldn't be in a huge hurry to seek her out. He'd been talking to Miguel in the library. To explain the silver teapot, the sandwiches and cake, his uncle would have given him the information that she was due to join him at any moment. So he was probably still there, lounging back in the leather chair opposite the desk his uncle was using, drinking tea and looking forward to telling her she was dumped. Moving on with the rest of his gold-plated life!

Scuttling down the long and empty corridor, down the service staircase, avoiding the main living quarters, she made it to the kitchens. There was usually someone around, even at this quiet time of day, and several of the staff spoke her language. During Cayo's absence, with Miguel's help, she'd been trying to get her head round the basics of theirs. So she'd get by. Just about.

But the cavernous room was empty and silent. Most of the staff lived in, and she should have known they would be relaxing in their rooms or taking advantage of the custom-made gym and swimming pool in the extensive cellar region at this time of day.

Swallowing a frustrated sob, she darted out to the service courtyard, in the forlorn hope of finding someone still busy with some sort of duty. Immediately she spied Rodolfo, sprawled out on a bench in the shade, his nose in a newspaper.

Sending up a prayer of thankfulness for her deliverance, she pulled in a deep, hopefully calming breath and approached him, forcing herself to smile, because he was frowning at her horribly puffy reddened eyes.

'Are you busy?' Obviously he wasn't, but she felt it only polite to ask.

'No, *señorita*. May I help you?'

'I need a lift to the nearest town.'

'A lift?'

He was wrinkling his eyes. Clearly his knowledge of English didn't stretch that far.

'Someone to drive me to the nearest town or village.'

She didn't care where. All she cared about was putting distance between herself and the man who had so cruelly used and betrayed her, taken advantage of her deplorable naïvety. Feeling herself on the brink of tears, she forced her mouth to smile again. And felt weak with relief when he finally understood, folded his newspaper and got to his feet.

'Certainly, *señorita*, if it is possible. If the car for the staff is not in use, then I will drive you where you like. I will see.'

Watching him walk across the courtyard to the row of garages, Izzy held her breath. The appointed time for English afternoon tea was well and truly over. Had Miguel sent Cayo to look for her? Or roused the housekeeper? In either event, her letter would have been found.

How would Cayo explain the contents of the note to his uncle? Perhaps he wouldn't. Would just say she'd left. But Miguel cared about her. He'd insist she was found, question the staff. Any minute now a search party might explode into this courtyard, and she'd be forced to explain herself.

She couldn't face Cayo. She never wanted to have to lay eyes on him again. It would hurt more than her poor battered heart could bear!

Rodolfo had opened the doors of the farthest garage and disappeared inside. To her tortured mind he seemed to have been out of sight for weeks instead of seconds. When she heard the well-bred purr of an engine she sagged with relief, and expelled the breath she hadn't realised she was holding. She had to force herself to stay where she was and not fly over the cobbles and fling herself into the slowly emerging sleek black car.

When the vehicle eventually sighed to a halt beside her, she made herself stand still while

Rodolfo exited, all smiles, and paced round to open the rear door. Then, unable to contain herself a second longer, she was flinging the rucksack on the back seat and was into the front passenger seat before he could blink, fastening the seat belt with hands that felt like a dozen fat fumbling thumbs.

'You want shops?' The chef's assistant still looked puzzled.

Izzy decided hysterically that he probably thought she was unhinged, so she made her voice flat and level as she countered, 'No, I just want to explore a little while I am in your beautiful country.' Inside her head she was screaming, *Go! Go! Go!* But she invented, with a calmness that deeply amazed her, 'I'll find somewhere to stay for two or three nights and phone when I want to return to Las Palomas.'

Which would be never.

Rodolfo shrugged, slanting her a long, assessing look. Praying he didn't find her story so thin he'd feel duty-bound to check with his employers, Izzy said tightly, 'I *am* permitted time out to do my own thing.'

'Then Arcos, I think. Not too far—an hour to drive. It is a beautiful town, one of the *pueblos blancos*, high on a rock, with a river running round and many places to stay—'

'Sounds perfect,' Izzy said through her teeth. She didn't need the tourist spiel. She would only be in the town for as long as it took to hire a taxi to take her some place else—back to the coast, where, hopefully, she would find work. 'Let's go, shall we?'

As Rodolfo complied, poker-faced, and the car purred towards the wide archway in the stout stone walls, Izzy didn't know how she managed to sit still. She only began to relax just a little when they were on the narrow, winding mountain road, and tried for a whole two seconds at a time to put her disastrous immediate past behind her.

Her uncertain future was something she was going to have to think about when she'd got herself together again—had stopped wanting to rant and rave and throw things and give Cayo Garcia a black eye that would keep him hiding behind shades for weeks, wanting to cry herself sick because she was hurting so badly.

Ten minutes into the journey, Izzy was sinking into a pit of such deep misery she didn't know how she was ever going to climb out of it. The imperious buzz of the in-car phone didn't make an impression until Rodolfo brought the car to a halt on a bend that overhung one of the scariest precipices she had ever seen.

'I must answer this.'

The young chef's assistant unhooked the instrument, listened more than he spoke. Izzy, her brow furrowing, could pick out the affirmatives but little else of the rapid Spanish interchange.

When the call ended he turned big soulful eyes on her. He looked chastened. 'That was *el patrón*,' he told her. 'We are to wait here until he comes.'

Izzy felt distinctly nauseous as her stomach

jumped into her throat. 'Cayo?' She could hardly get his name past her shock-frozen lips.

'*Sí*. There is to be trouble.'

CHAPTER FOURTEEN

RAGE was consuming Cayo with a rare ferocity as he swung out of his car and approached the young man standing on the hot, dusty road, his face greenish beneath the olive-toned skin.

Tight-lipped, he issued terse instructions, then swung round and opened the door at Izzy's side. 'Out!'

She didn't look at him, he noted with dark wrathful eyes. Something had happened. He intended to find out what. He watched with barely contained impatience as she left the vehicle with obvious reluctance, her body stiff, her soft mouth set. She looked as if she were about to explode. Having been on the receiving end of her tirades in the past, he waited grimly.

It didn't happen. Like a poorly articulated puppet she allowed him to deposit her in the passenger seat of his car. She said nothing as he started the engine and drove at speed to where the narrow road flattened slightly and widened, permitting him to turn. He checked in his mirror that Rodolfo was following as instructed.

Izzy kept her eyes firmly on the window at her side, seeing nothing. Her heart was thumping. She couldn't look at him. If she did she would totally lose it. As it was, she was holding on to her self-control for grim life.

Clearly he was furious. He must have found her note, read it. It would have taken his analytical brain only one second to send him to check on the garages, to find the car the staff had the use of missing, punch in the numbers of the car phone—and bingo!

Though why he had bothered to drag her back she was too distraught to even begin to fathom. Asked to second-guess his reaction, she would have said that he must have tossed the note aside, shrugged his impressively wide shoulders and considered himself fortunate in being spared her possible recriminations. Or, worse, the unedifying spectacle of a female in messy, noisy tears when he told her he'd changed his mind on the subject of marriage.

Unless, of course, his head was so monumentally huge he couldn't stomach the idea of being given the heave-ho. *He* did the loving and leaving—not the other way round! It had to be a first for him. And he didn't like it. It made him furious.

In that moment she was sure she absolutely hated him. Staring fixedly ahead, she clipped out through a jaw that felt as if it had been set in concrete, 'Don't take your fit of pique out on Rodolfo. He was only following my instructions.' And then she shut up, before the lump in her throat choked her.

'And I intend to discover why you gave those instructions,' he came right back at her as he brought the car to a halt in the inner courtyard.

An impatient stride brought him to where she sat, her neck and shoulders aching with tension

On legs that felt as if they would give way at any moment, Izzy found herself being virtually frogmarched through the impressive main entrance. His fingers bit like a vice into her arm, and he merely dipped his head in cursory acknowledgement of the housekeeper who was refreshing the flower arrangements in the vast main hall. He totally ignored what sounded like some pleasantry coming from the portly woman, sweeping Izzy up the great stone staircase and depositing her in the room she had never expected to enter again.

The silence stung and lengthened unbearably. Reflecting that she was such a failure she couldn't even manage an escape bid without being ignominiously hauled back, and with what passed as her pride in ragged tatters, Izzy swallowed a sob.

Cayo said, with a gentleness that shocked her rigid, 'Why did you write this?'

For the first time her eyes swung to him. Widened. He was holding the note she'd scribbled in such haste. Her heart twisted inside her breast. He'd discarded the jacket of his suit, and his white shirt was open at the base of his tanned throat, tucked into the waistband of his narrow-fitting trousers, dark grey this time. He looked, as always, utterly sensational.

Izzy trembled with the impact, but, straightening her already tense shoulders, told herself with iron determination that she wasn't going to let herself get all moony and feeble over a man who was clearly an out-and-out louse. 'I would have thought it was clear enough,' she uttered thinly.

And he smiled—actually had the gall to smile!—and gave a negative shake of his far-too-handsome head, which sent a lock of his so touchable dark hair tumbling over his forehead.

It made her treacherous fingers ache to push it back, but she puffed out her chest and yelled, 'I don't want to marry you! I *won't*! Can't you understand something that simple?' She was almost hopping on the spot she was so plain cross—with him, with herself, with everything! 'You're just not used to having a marriage proposal flung in your face!' she spluttered.

'No.' His long, sensual mouth quirked unforgivably. 'I have never proposed marriage before, therefore I am a stranger to a refusal.' A graceful stride brought him close enough to cup her chin, to lift her face so that he could look deeply into her wide and now frantic eyes. 'Tell me what is wrong, my Isabella.'

When he used that intimate tone, employed the Spanish version of her name, she always melted in a puddle of goo. Now was no different.

'Don't!' She twisted her head away.

'Don't do what?' He captured her chin again, his thumb stroking her taut jawline. 'This? Touch you?' Taking her strangled groan as confirmation, he delivered, 'The words I read are not those of the woman I have come to know and love—'

That was too much! *Way* too much! 'Don't

you *dare* say that!' she exploded, pummelling his all too solid chest with ineffectual fists.

What was the tricky devil planning? To soft-talk her into bed with him again? To use that magnetic personality, that hypnotic sex appeal, those shatteringly charismatic good-looks, to turn her into a mindless slave all over again? And then, when he considered he'd got his just revenge for her crass impertinence in turning him down, to show her the door?

That wasn't going to happen! Unaccustomed as he was to anyone going against his wishes, this time he would find he'd met his match!

'Don't say what?' He caught her flailing fists between his strong hands, jerking her closer, so that she could feel his body heat, smell his tantalising male scent: fresh air, a faint aroma of lemony cologne. She trembled as he murmured, 'That I love you?'

Closing her eyes and pretending that being this close to him turned her stomach wasn't working. By anyone's reckoning he would come top of the seduction stakes—by a mile—in any league table! So she relaunched into attack mode, huge blue eyes brimming with withering scorn.

'Go to the top of the class! I asked you to tell me that once. You couldn't bring yourself to say it! Just blithered on about loving my body!'

He brought his head down to hers, nuzzling against her ear. His voice was soft with amusement as he told her, 'I didn't know I blithered. I must be getting old! Perhaps I should be careful not to start dribbling, too.'

Definitely against her better judgement, Izzy wanted to giggle.

He said, really soberly, 'I fudged it because I'm a fool. I'd been falling in love with you for weeks, but I was too set against allowing that I could, or ever would, give my future happiness into the hands of any woman to see it.'

Izzy would have given twenty years of her life to be able to believe him! The physical craving to melt into him, to lift her face for his kiss, was torture. But she was going to resist it with all her might.

She was so entangled with her inner battle that before she knew it she'd been led to the fancy empire-style sofa that stood beneath one of the tall windows that marched along the outer bedroom wall.

Cayo angled his lean and superb body beside her, his brilliant eyes narrowed on her pale features, and his voice was like an exquisite physical caress as he relayed, 'When I found that note I was furious enough to pull down the castle walls with my bare hands. Then my brain took over and told me that it made no kind of sense. Something had happened to make a sweet, loving woman on the brink of marriage run from the man she loved.'

His gentle smile, the soft touch of his hand as it briefly closed on hers, sent her into a tailspin.

'Tell me why a woman who'd work for next to nothing to care for an elderly man who, or so she believed, was severely impoverished, who would pass up the opportunity of acquiring an expensive new wardrobe to rescue a stray dog, a generously spirited woman with a heart as big as a bucket, a woman who'd think nothing about saying what she thought, shouting the odds if she felt an injustice had been done, would sneak away and leave such a vicious letter for the man she loves? It is not in character, my Isabella. So tell me the truth.'

She was going to cry!

No—no, she wasn't!

He couldn't blind her with soft soap! She knew the truth—knew what he was really like. He'd condemned himself within her hearing.

'You won't like this,' she pointed out. A man like Cayo Angel Garcia—a big shot in the world of business, top dog in all other spheres of his life—would hate having his shortcoming thrust under his handsome nose. 'You'd been away for longer than you'd said you would be. I was missing you,' she confessed. She'd lost everything when she'd heard the truth, so she might as well lose the last tattered rag of her pride. 'I heard you talking to Miguel and I was ecstatic. You were home. When I heard what you were saying I—' Her eyes flooded with despised tears. Reliving the nightmare brought her loss back to her with hideously savage reality.

'What I was saying?' Cayo prompted swiftly, a frown indenting his smooth brow as he watched the slow fall of her tears.

Furiously swiping at the wetness on her cheeks with the tips of her fingers, she lowered her head. She didn't want him to see the pain she was sure she wouldn't be able to hide. It hurt so badly to remember his words. So much more to actually repeat them. 'You were telling your uncle that you were anti-marriage, saying a man would be a fool to settle for one flower when he could flit from one to the other without losing his freedom.'

Having been found out in his duplicity, Izzy had fully expected him either to bluster or simply shrug and walk away. She certainly didn't expect his lazy reply. 'Do you always act like a headless chicken when faced with a crisis? Didn't it cross your mind to speak to me? Tell me what you thought you'd heard?'

Being compared to a headless chicken was just too much! She'd been called a brainless blond bimbo, a nuisance and a failure, and had taken it on the chin. But a headless chicken!

Her head snapped up, and she met his amused dark gaze with blue shards of ice. 'I didn't want you to see how much you'd hurt me,' she stated between gritted teeth. And if he started to gloat at that snippet of information she would hit him into next week! 'I heard what I heard. I didn't dream it up!'

'Sheath your claws, *amada*.' He reached forward, placed strong warm hands on her tiny waist and dragged her against the curve of his body.

Desire tugged at her. She resisted it, made herself rigid as a plank of wood, staring fixedly at the painting of a bowl of old-fashioned roses on the opposite wall. One of the blooms had fallen onto a light grey velvet cloth, like a dew-filmed deep red jewel. She told herself that she would never understand him in a million years. Having been found out, he should be making arrangements for her permanent and immediate removal. Not this. Whatever *this* was.

'Had you arrived a few moments earlier, or listened just a little longer, you would have heard what I really said.'

His dark head was so close to hers now. If she turned they would be touching. Her forehead against the side of his jaw…

Keep staring at the painting!

'My uncle can get tedious on the subject of my settling down and raising a family. Not having experienced a loving family life—just a father who could hardly bear to look at me, a series of tutors and then a rigidly strict boarding school—I convinced myself early on that I could stand alone. Besides, I believed I was incapable of wholehearted, unconditional love. I was a complete stranger to such an emotion,' he told her frankly. 'This afternoon I reminded Miguel of what my past and admittedly flippant response had always been, but I went on to tell him that, to his doubtless relief, I'd met a woman who had changed my mind.'

The temptation to believe him was strong enough to have her redoubling her efforts to remain totally unyielding. Until the flaw in his explanation hit her. She turned then, and glared at him, her words fizzing. 'Huh! So what happened to keeping the whole thing a deathly secret until we'd spoken to my family? Written in stone, that was! Forget your own strict orders, did you?'

Utilising the best way he knew to stop her yelling at him, Cayo covered her lips with his own, hauling her suddenly boneless body closer. He was already so hot for her he didn't know what to do with himself, but with aching reluctance he dragged his mouth from the heady invitation of hers and managed thickly,

'I didn't tell him who the woman was, only that I had met her. I still feel your family should be the first to be told. You have to believe me— believe that I love you, that I want you with me for the rest of my life, that I want to give you my children, to wake every morning with you at my side, to the sunshine you bring with you. Tell me you want that, too. Tell me you love me. I can't be happy without you.'

At the first intoxicating touch of his lips on hers she had been lost all over again, giddy and boneless, clinging to his broad shoulders with atavistic longing. And at his final words she knew she could believe him—trust him with her life and happiness.

Lifting one hand, she tenderly laid it against the side of his lean dark face, feeling the incipient stubble on his tough jaw, and spoke the words he wanted to hear through lips that felt swollen and ravaged from the unapologetic urgency of his kiss. She saw his dark eyes glitter with shameless male satisfaction.

He turned his mouth into the palm of her hand, and she loved the feeling so much that she had to reach up and cover the underside of his jaw with delirious kisses—until he gave a feral groan and took her face between his hands, his voice not quite steady as he said, in a tone that coming from any other man on the planet Izzy would have described as pleading, 'You will marry me?'

'Just try to stop me!' Not the most romantic response, as she would be the first to admit— but, hey, she was so ecstatic she hardly knew what she was saying.

When he dropped a kiss on the tip of her nose and said, 'So all is forgiven?' she could only giggle.

'Even the headless chicken insult!' she responded.

'Ah! Such a beautiful head, my Isabella.' Lingeringly, he ran his fingers through her untameable hair, and looked as if he was enjoying the sensation just as much as she was. 'An excusable reaction, under the circumstances. One I can fully relate to. When I read that note and thought I'd lost the one love of my life I was ready, for a few moments that are best forgotten, to do terminal damage to anyone or anything I laid my eyes on.'

'That bad, was it?' Izzy snuggled closer. She was the happiest woman ever to live.

Somehow or other her legs had got themselves hooked over his lap, and his hand that wasn't tucked very snugly around her waist was stroking the curve of her jeans-clad thigh with intent.

'I prefer you in skirts, *mi amada.*' He gave her the smile that always sent her off the planet. 'It is a crime to hide such lovely legs, such warm and generous thighs. But…' He vented a sigh that sounded as if it came from the soles of his feet. 'Tough stuff first.' He swung her to her feet and took one of her hands in his. 'Come. We phone your family, issue wedding invitations, and then break our news to Miguel—who will, understandably but frustratingly, insist on a celebratory dinner.' He lifted her hand to his lips, playing havoc with her ability to stand. 'It will be tough getting through the hours before I can have you to myself. I think, *mi amada*, I might go a little crazy!'

As the helicopter began its descent Izzy clutched Cayo's hand even more tightly. To take her mind off the tummy-churning sensation, she reflected dreamily on her wedding day.

It had been as perfect as it could get. A simple ceremony in the tiny village church—low key, to keep the paparazzi in the dark, Cayo had explained. He had a high media profile, and he refused to have that mob spoil their day. Then a sumptuous reception back at the castle, with all the staff invited along with what seemed like the cream of high-bred Spanish society.

She hadn't been fazed, though. Everyone had been lovely to her, and the language barrier no longer existed—or not really. Cayo had been proud of her attempts and had helped her with enthusiasm. Now she could converse with anyone, with only the occasional slip, which often gave her the giggles when her error was gently explained to her.

Her dad had looked proud of her as he'd walked her up the aisle, and her mother had beamed as if her hitherto trial of a daughter had done something right for the first time in her life. Even James had unbent sufficiently to give her an awkward hug, and his brainy wife had kissed her on both cheeks.

The four of them were to stay at Las Palomas for a short holiday with Miguel, who had pronounced himself delighted that this day had dawned, and had made a long, erudite speech to that effect, intimating that he'd known all along that she was the perfect wife for his picky nephew.

Even Benji had worn a white satin ribbon on his collar in honour of the occasion, and had been fed so many tidbits that he'd fallen asleep in a snoring heap on Miguel's lap.

The reception had still been in full, enjoyable swing when Cayo had plucked her out of the throng and carried her through the courtyard to where a limousine had been waiting to take them to the airport.

'I have already waited too long to have my new bride to myself,' he had murmured as he'd settled her on the rear seat, slid in beside her and closed the shaded glass partition between them and the driver. 'Now I shall make up for wasted time,' he'd vowed, removing her veil. And he had proceeded to kiss her senseless.

And now, after a night flight to Athens in his private jet and a short helicopter ride, they were circling an island, thickly wooded in places, with a tiny village bunched around a harbour. The rocky coastline admitted a few white-sanded coves, and there was a sprawling white mansion surrounded by smooth lawns and what looked like a really dreamy garden flowing down to meet a fern-covered ravine that led to a beach.

'It's so beautiful,' Izzy breathed as they touched down, entranced by what she saw. She gave her brand-new husband a radiant smile. 'Thank you for keeping our honeymoon destination secret. If I'd known we were coming to a Greek island I'd have been imagining what it would look like. Now it's a lovely surprise.'

'And it's yours,' Cayo supplied with his mesmerising smile as he lifted her out of the craft, setting her on her feet as he turned to speak to the pilot about unloading their gear.

Smoothing down the skirts of her fabulous wedding dress—layers of the softest creamy lace over ivory silk, with a fitted bodice embroidered with seed pearls and the narrowest of sleeves, ending in a point just above her broad gold wedding band and the frankly enormous diamond Cayo had slipped on her finger after the ceremony—she watched with adoring eyes as he strode back to her.

Dawn had been breaking when they'd left Athens, and now the early morning shimmered, fresh and clear. Izzy, her eyes wide with excitement, told him, 'My own honeymoon island for two whole months—how lovely!'

'Yours for ever, wife!' He swept her up in his arms and began to stride towards the white villa.

Izzy, clutching at her trailing skirts with one hand, the other curled around the nape of his neck, said, sounding stunned, 'This is all mine? I can't believe it!'

'When I left you for a few days I was in Athens, pushing through the details. The owner wanted a quick sale—lock, stock and barrel. I didn't tell you what I was doing. I wanted it to be a surprise.'

'Oh, my!' She kissed him with an enthusiasm that stopped him in his tracks. 'What have I done to deserve you?'

'Simply been your own beautiful, loving self,' he answered on a husky growl.

He carried her over the threshold into a cool marble-floored living space, with gauzy curtains fluttering in the breeze from the high arched windows, delicate apricot-coloured walls and comfy-looking sofas covered in cream linen.

Wide glass doors opened onto a stone terrace overlooking the sea, and the kitchen was a dream. Even the bathrooms were a miracle of marble and glass.

'It's perfect!' Izzy breathed excitedly as Cayo set her on her feet in the master bedroom and kissed her smiling mouth. 'Will we be able to come here often?'

'Often,' he promised, beginning to slip the tiny buttons at the back of her wedding dress from their moorings. 'I can do most of my work from Las Palomas, but here will be our retreat. Our special paradise.' His eyes glimmered as he slid the dress from her slender shoulders. 'A couple from the village come each day to attend to the house and gardens—you will meet them later. But first, we will share a shower, and then…'

He ran his hands over her tingling, luscious breasts and shimmied the dress from her curvy hips until it pooled at her feet on the floor, leaving her in just a tiny pair of silk panties.

'You looked beautiful in your wedding gown,' he said on an audible intake of breath, 'but you look even more beautiful without it.' And he plundered her eager mouth until she was shaking with anticipation.

Her only thought, rapidly dwindling in coherence, was that she had her own surprise for him.

In their late-night discussions he had confided that he wanted children.

And she was pregnant. Their child would be her gift to him. That and her eternal, adoring love.

MILLS & BOON PUBLISH EIGHT LARGE PRINT TITLES A MONTH. THESE ARE THE EIGHT TITLES FOR MAY 2009.

☙

THE BILLIONAIRE'S BRIDE OF VENGEANCE
Miranda Lee

THE SANTANGELI MARRIAGE
Sara Craven

THE SPANIARD'S VIRGIN HOUSEKEEPER
Diana Hamilton

THE GREEK TYCOON'S RELUCTANT BRIDE
Kate Hewitt

NANNY TO THE BILLIONAIRE'S SON
Barbara McMahon

CINDERELLA AND THE SHEIKH
Natasha Oakley

PROMOTED: SECRETARY TO BRIDE!
Jennie Adams

THE BLACK SHEEP'S PROPOSAL
Patricia Thayer

 MILLS & BOON®
Pure reading pleasure™